GROWING UP IN THE COLD WAR

CODE NAME: KITTEN

CATHY O'BRYAN

GROWING UP IN THE COLD WAR
CODE NAME KITTEN, BOOK 2

Copyright © 2020 Cathy O'Bryan

All rights reserved. Except for use in any review, the reproduction or utilization of this work in whole or in part in any form by any electronic, mechanical or other means, now known or hereinafter invented, including xerography, photocopying and recording, or in any information storage or retrieval system, is forbidden without the written permission of the publisher.

This is a work of fiction. Names, characters, places and incidents are either the product of the author's imagination or are used fictitiously, and any resemblance to actual persons, living or dead, business establishments, events or locales is entirely coincidental.

Printed in the USA.

DEDICATION

This series of books would not be possible without my parents and family's influence. My Dan and my children Laura and Dan have supported me all the way. Robin and Madison listened and kept me on the right path.

To all my friends and family, thank you seems small in comparison to the support given but "Thank you".

ONE

It's Over

THE BUS ACCIDENT IS A mess. It wasn't an accident; we were targeted.

The other two buses that were not involved made it safely to the hotel. Needless to say, they were worried when we all disappeared.

Of course, we haven't really disappeared. We're all over the highway. One motor coach, four security Suburbans, one limo, two bad guy cars and a butt load of police, military personnel and ambulances, plus a morgue van are sitting in the median. People, debris and news teams are spread out everywhere. The traffic is backed up as far as I can see in both directions. People are out of their cars and milling around. Safe to say, it is a zoo.

TWO

Langley OPS

- Florida teams have their hands full with the accident.
- Local police are assisting.
- The story for the media is being worked on as we speak.
- One civilian death in bus three.
- Two serious civilian injuries are being transported to Miami by medical helicopter.
- Other minor injuries being treated by local EMT on-site.
- Four perp fatalities.
- Two prisoners.
- Two Black Hawks from MacDill Air Force Base with military special teams aboard will assist in the extraction of prisoners and assets.
- Whitey and Kitten are on their way to the base with their team.
- Big Bird will be in the air soon to MacDill.
- Our Langley team will be on the ground at the base in less than two hours.

THREE

MacDill Air Force Base

DAD'S LIMO APPEARED TO BE okay, but the two Suburbans that had pulled next to it have evidence of a gunfight. The bullet holes can't be hidden. Dad said Caesar and company were already in the air to MacDill Air Force Base near Tampa. I could see a huge military helicopter just down the median to my right and a MEDEVAC helicopter took off from the median to my left. The side says Life Flight. Who is in that? I have never seen a helicopter like that in person, but I know Houston has one at their medical center. I guess Miami has one, too. Seconds later, the big military helicopter takes off, revealing another just a few yards away in the median. The noise of the two choppers just adds to the mayhem on the ground.

The traffic jam is monumental. I'm grateful that I'm safe and uninjured, apart from a few bruises. Charlie grabs my hand and leads the way to the other big chopper waiting farther down the median. Sterling, Marty, Sean, and Dad are close behind. As we get closer, I wonder if Eddie has ever been in one of these. This machine is scary. It was one of those really big, ugly ones you see on the news. You know the ones they use in Vietnam, very, very scary-looking the closer you get. The wind it generates islike a hurricane. My hair is swirling around so much I have to hold onto it just to see where I am going, not to mention to keep it from getting hopelessly tangled. We approach it anyway. Charlie, with me in tow, duck and begin to run to get out of this field of debris from the chopper. As I get to the open door, hands reach for me and I fly right in. I feel like a fairy. I'm still dressed from the game in my cougar costume, all I need is wings. My costume is a form-fitting bodysuit, a black nose, tail and whiskers. I look ridiculous and out of place. I get a few raised eyebrows from the men inside. As I am being strapped in my seat, I am also fitted with headphones. What a relief! The headphones cancel out the amazing noise of the chopper. Charlie, Sterling, Marty, Sean, and Dad are not talkative. All I see are just cold stares as they are somewhere else. After everyone is aboard and harnessed in, we're off to MacDill Air Force Base. I can hear the pilots talking to each other about take-off info through my headphones. I bet everyone else can hear, too.

I can see Dad, Sean, Marty, Sterling and, of course, Charlie. Charlie is harnessed next to me. This chopper ride is a first for me and it is exhilarating and daunting all in one. I am glad to have Charlie's hand. All of the other passengers are openly armed and ready for anything, they are SWAT-like. They are all men and no one even looks my way, except Dad. I smile as our eyes meet and I blow him a kiss. We have made it. Caesar is in custody.... captured. What a relief. But where is Mike?

I lean into Charlie and ask "Where's Mike?"

He points to the headgear we have on and I realize there is a mic attached to my headset, too. After a moment of feeling around, I find the mic button. This is a nice toy, and I decide to play with the toy they've given me.

Into the mic, I said, "Pardon me all you beautiful men, but this conversation is for my Dad."

Eleven lovely pairs of eyes immediately stare at me. It is empowering. As I scan the group, all have soft eyes pivoted toward me but no one smiles. That should have clued me in to be quiet, but no, I continue. Dad did not have soft eyes, his were blazing. I ignore the burning hole being focused on me by Dad. Making sure everyone knew who I was addressing, I say "Where is Mike, Dad?"

His answer was delivered in a measured voice, "Mike took Caesar ahead in the other military chopper."

I can tell I should just thank him and shut up, but I just can't. I am so relieved that we have the bad guys and that my world might just be normal again. I'm feeling liberated. "So, Dad, since we got Caesar why do we need all of this gorgeous manpower strapped in with us?"

Six soldiers cut their eyes in my direction and sort of smirk. Charlie stiffens. Sean, Sterling, and Marty cringe, and Dad, well he did the Dad thing and glares at me. Then he spoke.

"I believe they are here to protect all of us. These men are highly qualified soldiers, not eye candy for my teenage daughter." Ok, that shut me up. Like I said, I should have thanked them and just shut up. Charlie squeezes my hand in support and smiles down at me.

What next? Is this really over? I want to ask a million questions, but the look on Dad's face gives me pause... no, actually, I just need to stop talking altogether. I sit back and take in the sights and allow my body to lean into Charlie. He presses back. I do my best not to moan at this touch; Charlie feels wonderful.

The apprehension of Caesar and his crew, is it a factor in any political activity in Washington, or is this just clean up from WWII? I have no idea. I have never really paid much attention to the politics surrounding me other than elections and only then to attend rallies that my parents attended. It is time for a change.

Haven't you always heard people say 'it's a need to know thing'? Well, this girl needs to know.

We land and I have the pleasure of jumping out into Charlie's arms. When we walk far enough away from the chopper, I am surprised again when no one will talk to me. Everyone I address is silent. Dad notices.

Dad said, "You need to be debriefed first before anyone can talk to you besides me."

"Huh, what? Me, why me?" I look at Dad's serious face and chide back "ok, let's get this done."

"That's my girl, get business done before personal needs. You are such a trooper," he says proudly, smiling.

I just stare. I am not a trooper, I just have many questions. A debriefing sounds like a good place to get that done.

On the ground, I see Charlie step aside and disappear with the guys and Dad says to follow. We end up in some sort of residence.

"Where are we? What is this place?"

I look around and see the luggage that I had left in the hotel in Miami.

"Is this my room?"

"Yes, it is our quarters for now. Take a shower, get dressed, dinner is at 1930," Dad says.

I'm confused. "What about debriefing?"

He smiles that sorry-you-don't-get-it smile and says, "That's at 2030 back at headquarters."

I nod. Ok. I'm dirty, still in costume and an overall mess, so a shower sounds good. I have 30 minutes to get ready. So, 15 minutes in the shower and 15 for the rest. Thank God I'm not high maintenance.

I'm ready to go with two minutes to spare, go me. Dad is not a man to be late for. I'm wearing jeans, a T-shirt and a light jacket. It is nice outside. Even in December, Florida has nice weather, kind of like Houston.

Dad and I walk to the Officer's mess hall. My boys are not there. It seems so surreal, after all this time with them, to not have them by my side.

Dad looks at me sort of sideways. "What are you looking for? Caesar is in a cage, it's ok."

I jump. I hadn't even thought of him.

Dinner smells wonderful. I didn't realize I'm hungry until the smell came blasting out of the door. I order a steak, mashed potatoes and carrots, and it is delightful. Dad seems to be a little more relaxed after dinner.

FOUR

LANGLEY OPS

- Kitten, Big Bird and Whitey are being housed at MacDill AFB for debriefing.
- Other assigned agents on the ground during the capture are on their way here for debriefing.
- They should arrive at 0100 and begin debrief at 0800.
- Tiger is at Patuxent River Naval Station.

FIVE

Debriefing

———

AT 2020, DAD AND I BEGIN our walk to HQ for the debriefing. My mind wonders what could I know that would help. I was in the motor coach. Yes, I saw the bad guy's cars cut off our bus, but right after that the bus rolled on its side and slid.

I never saw Caesar at all, which made me quite happy. Well, here goes nothing. I'm led to a small room with two agents. Unhappily, I'm alone for this. I would have loved for Charlie to just sit with me, or even Dad. I have watched enough TV and movies that I am sure I know how this is going. Boy, am I wrong. The two men introduce themselves as Phil, a big German-looking guy, and Antonio, who is Hispanic. They point at the camera that has a blinking red light and the big mirror. Ok, so the camera is recording and the big mirror must be a two-way mirror. Hmmm, who is watching? Maybe Dad. I sit back and wait.

Phil smiles and says, "So, tell us about the gardenias."

I am stunned. There were no gardenias today and I say so.

Phil smiles again and Antonio speaks. "We mean in the hospital after the explosion."

I am startled, I guess. "Ok, I can tell you that. It was a little creepy. I was kinda drugged up and this dark-haired young man bent over me and tells me everything is ok. He kisses me on the forehead. I thought it was a dream until I saw the little gardenia plant on the table next to my bed. Next to the plant is a cute teddy bear. It is different than the one that was there the day before, but cute. Sean took both away in bags. Sean also swabbed my forehead. That scared me most." Whew, that wasn't as easy as I thought.

"When you rolled downhill at Johns Hopkins, did the man seem familiar," Phil asked.

I look up and sigh. This is not what I thought they wanted to know. I think back to that scary moment. When I think about it now, I do feel like I knew him. Not by looking at him but by smell. It was his cologne, I think.

I tell Phil and Antonio just that. "I mean, I didn't make the connection until much later. At the time, I was busy fighting for my life. And he punched me out."

Phil nods and then says, "Tell us how and when you met Caesar."

This is easy. "I met him in Spain at Carlos Ramos' house. I met Carlos' parents and two sisters and Caesar." They all had seemed like a nice family.

Antonio says, "So, how did they introduce him? As family, as a family-friend, or just Carlos' friend?"

"Well, Carlos and Caesar seemed to be close friends and Carlos' father treated Caesar with the respect of an equal. The others seemed to just be there. At the time I was nervous, but not frightened." I said.

This went on, and on, and on. I am exhausted. I decided to put my head down on the table to rest.

The door opens a second later with my Dad saying, "That's enough for now."

I get up to go with him when Phil says, "We have more questions for her. A lot more."

I have reached Dad and feel safe.

He quietly says, "Tomorrow is another day. Good night gentlemen."

I love my Dad. We walk back to our rooms and I fall into bed. Yes, tomorrow will be another day... Hopefully, just a little slower.

To my surprise, my Mom is there at breakfast. I couldn't believe my eyes. I blinked twice just to be sure. Mom looked tired, but ready for anything. She looked like she was ready to attack anyone asking for it. I begin approaching cautiously, but knowing I haven't done anything wrong, or at least I don't think so, I run over and hug her.

"When did you get in? I thought Dad and I were catching up with you and Lucy for Christmas in D.C.?"

She smiles and says, "Lucy and I were there. I left her with Susan and Linda. I got in last night in time to snuggle with your Dad and then catch some sleep." I am sure Lucy was happy with my crazy first cousins, who are not my favorite people. Lucy loves being with them.

Mom and Dad were looking at each other and smiling like kids who had just had sex. Yikes, I shouldn't think like that. They have always looked at each other with a deep understanding of love. Just lately I've begun noticing their body language suggests intimacy. I hope when I get old like them, I have that kind of relationship... love and lust.

"After talking to your Dad last night, I thought you might need me here to keep the interrogators in line." I nod, I am just happy she is here. I lean over and hug her again.

I order breakfast happily. I'm pleased both of my parents are here and focused on me. Mom has pancakes, Dad his usual two eggs over easy, bacon, and toast, my go-to breakfast, too. Mom allows breakfast to end before she quizzes me, which I'm grateful for.

As they clear the table she says, "So tell me about Phil and Antonio."

"Well, both were nice and polite but the hours of questions and the long day were too much. I needed sleep. They asked about things that happened four years ago. The retelling was good because I had new insight, but I was so tired. I remember Dad leading me out and a short walk but I don't remember getting into a nightgown."

I lean back with my orange juice glass in hand to think about yesterday. It was not just long but crazy. My day that started with a football game, ended with a bus accident, a helicopter ride, a delicious dinner and a three-hour debriefing. I sure hope today will be slower. As I put my glass down, Mom is waving her hands in front of me and speaking.

"Are you listening?"

" I'm back," I say. "Sorry, I zoned out."

Mom sighs and says for the second time, "That kind of debriefing will not happen again."

I am happy that Mom is on the scene. Wait, what? I have to do that again?

"I have to do that again?" I ask out loud.

Mom looks at me sad-like and says, "Yes, for a little while. I will be in the room this time. Your Dad can't because he is being debriefed, too. He is part of it, but not me."

"Let's get this over with," Dad says.

With that, we are up and on our way to HQ. HQ is busier than yesterday, and that is saying a lot. The headquarters is in your typical military building. Everyone seems to have a purpose in this building. Phil and Antonio appear out of nowhere, and you can see on their faces that Mom's presence is not what they want. Finally, we might have the upper hand.

My mom is amazing and sits right at my elbow. The questions begin... again, and briefly go over all four encounters with Caesar.

Mom stops them and asks, "Has it been confirmed that he was the perp all four times?"

Antonio replies, "The hospital visit after the bombing at your home was inconclusive, at first. Now that we have accurate fingerprints and blood samples, we can confirm he was in the hospital room with your daughter."

I can see Mom is shaken by this news. I don't blame her. It bothers me to think about it, too. I was alone with him. He could have wheeled me out of there without anyone knowing. I wonder why he didn't. The three of them discuss that back and forth. All I want is to make sure it is over, so I can be normal.

Antonio finally moves forward, and says, "The Johns Hopkins assault was confirmed with blood samples collected at the scene. The agent that fought with him bled also, so it took some serious lab time to separate and confirm. But again, we can confirm it was him. There is evidence of another, but no ID yet on that subject."

I am listening and my head is trying to process, but it is so overwhelming. Caesar spent a lot of time on me, but why?

Just thinking about what could have happened had he succeeded really spooks me.

Mom, on the other hand, is calm and steady as she continues. "What about exposure while she was in Spain?"

Phil talks this time. "We have been vetting and photographing all contacts, per your request. No one has jumped out as a threat in our surface investigation. It was a report that surfaced three weeks in that made us relook at Carlos Ramos again.... Well, really his father. That is when the Italian connection to the Rat Line surfaced. It wasn't hard to connect the dots and when we did, we extracted Emmy without consulting you first."

Wait, where was I all this time? I feel so stupid that I'm oblivious to my life. Well, the adult things in my world. I thought I was, I mean *am,* an adult. Obviously, I'm just brain dead.

Mom looks at me and says, "This is not a good time to zone out, Emmy. You need to listen and be aware."

I nod and I can see the sadness in her eyes.

"Why me and not Lucy?" I ask no one in particular.

Phil begins again, "we wondered that as well. After observing both of you, we discovered your sister isn't open to new people and travels with a close-knit group of rifle enthusiasts, which makes it more difficult to abduct her without a gun battle. Big risk there. You, on the other hand, have a wide range of friends and activities. You enjoy meeting new people, where she is very happy with her small close-knit group."

Wow, I guess I need to be boring and not talk to new people.

Mom must have read my mind and leaned and said, "That is one of my favorite things about you.... Your openness with new people and adventures."

I smile and just hug her.

Mom asks them to continue.

Phil starts again. "The fourth encounter, at the dorms in Houston, was their big plan. I guess they saw a great opportunity to get two at the same time. Our mistake was to room both you and Karly together. That made it an easy two-for-one hit."

Antonio chirps in, "Karly was as good a find as Emmy. Karly's dad is a senator and on several committees that also are in political play with South America and Cuba, like you and

Whitey."

I think Karly is nice and we were just getting to know each other when all this happened.

Antonio continues. "Their plan went sideways because they did not expect Emmy to fight and escape. That gave us some time to try to get ahead of them. We didn't completely get ahead of them, but with Emmy's help then and later, all ended well for the girls."

"I don't want to do that again, ever," I blurt out.

Mom, Antonio, and Phil turn and stare like they just remembered I was there. All three nod.

Mom begins, "So, that brings us to yesterday. What more do you need from her?"

Phil and Antonio look at each other, and back at Mom. Then Antonio says, "Well, I guess we are good for now. We like to be thorough."

I am more than ready to leave, so I stand.

Mom pulls me back down. "We, as a family, are going to allow Emmy to go back to Houston to school." I am stunned and grateful not to have to start over again. I like Houston.

"You can start that plan of action any time. When the holidays are over, we can sit down and hear your ideas. There is so much going on in South America, we will need to be there quite often, so I need a good plan to protect her."

Mom stops talking looking at both men for confirmation. I raise my hand then feeling like a fool for raising it like a kid in school and ask, "Why is it that I am a target? I mean, I don't know anything. I really didn't realize you guys were so important, sorry Mom, until recently."

Mom smiles, and says, "Dad and I are going to explain as much as possible over the holiday's.... It's time you understand." Both men sigh in relief and realize their job is over for now. They both stand and salute Mom and disappear.

SIX

Langley OPS

- Big Bird, Whitey, Kitten, and agent detail are on the way from Florida to Washington, D.C.
- Tiger will be in Washington for Christmas with family.
- Caesar and other prisoners are in custody and await a trail.
- Investigation is at a standstill in regards to associates helping Caesar.
- Texas agents will stay on duty with family for holidays while we work on Kitten's new Houston details.

SEVEN

Christmas

I LOVE WASHINGTON, D.C. AT CHRISTMAS TIME, IT'S beautiful. The tree at the White House is always beautiful and I love all the lights reflecting on the snow. Late at night, it's very mystical. I didn't get to go with the football team to Hawaii for the bowl game and I am really disappointed.

Being with Mom, Dad, Lucy and the boys are a great diversion. I'm sure later in life I will look back and wish I had gone, but no matter. 'It is what it is,' as Dad would say. My friends on the cheerleading squad and dance team sent me cards saying 'Get Well Soon'. Hmmm, I wonder what I have that kept me from going. I'll need to ask.

I thought Lucy would be in on the explanation of what Mom and Dad did, but she was out shopping. I guess the need-to-know comes in to play here, too. After what seems like all day of info, I decided to recap the high points to see if I have this down. The boys have all gone to their rooms or other assignments, so it is just Mom, Dad and me.

"Okay, let me see if I understand, Mom and Dad. Your assignment is as Naval attachés to the new Allende regime in Chile. I know things are heating up there and you two will be leaving soon. You two find Nazis, inform others about where they are and how to find them so they can be arrested by others and not you. You also go to Cuba and, I guess, fit into the social circles and listen and watch for clues about Nazis. Right?" I ask.

Mom explains, "Emmy, we are the attachés but we are CIA first. Now that you have heard that out loud, you need to forget it."

I just sit there and look at them. I guess I knew they did dangerous stuff but not being right there, it didn't seem real. It does now. This Caesar thing has changed that.

I nod to both so they know I heard them and understand.

Dad puts his arm on Mom and says, "I got this, Marie. As you can see Emmy, this upsets your Mom. She thought we could keep you and your sister out of this."

Dad waits a moment and starts with, "we have worked so hard to shelter you and Lucy from the world we are working hard to fix. Why did this man get so close? Where did the security go wrong?" he says to no one in particular.

"Wait, Dad. I'm the one who cultivated the friendship with Caesar. I didn't help this. Why didn't I see him for what he is?" I say. How embarrassing to admit my lack of awareness out loud.

I realize my Mom is patting my arm. I wonder why. "Did I miss something?"

Mom settles in and says, "Caesar has been trained all his life to be deceptive. He is really from Italy, his father is Italian and his mother is from Spain. He has both languages under control and sounds like a native in both. He was sent first to endear himself to Karly because her Dad was in Spain for an important meeting as a U.S. Senator. You appeared and there was a shift in focus to you. Your openness and friendliness were not your friends this time. Carlos, Caesar and their friends were at the Madrid airport when you all arrived as a group. They were fascinated by all the American girls, so they watched and listened. Red and Scarlet were his first conquests and that connection got them into your group. They helped with the luggage and from there, it was a piece of cake to hang out with all of you in Salamanca. Caesar had been at the hotel where Karly was staying, making that connection. He went to the airport to get Carlos and their friends because they had just come in from Italy. Karly thought Caesar had to go out of town for work or to visit family. She got quite attached to him, quickly. She was in Madrid and you were in Salamanca, not too far away. He found out who you are from Scarlet. She told Carlos that Dottie's father worked for NASA and your dad worked for the

U.S. government. I guess they did their homework and decided to try to keep both you and Karly as viable targets."

Mom took a breath and Dad moved in. "You asked what you could possibly know that he wanted?" I nod. "You didn't, and still don't, know much and he soon realized that. So, you became a candidate for kidnapping, for leverage. Karly, too."

"Okay, so the only way I was helpful was to take me and threaten you for info?" I asked.

Mom and Dad nod. "Well, maybe not info, but slow us down in our work."

"Okay I can deal with this, I think. What do you think I should know about Caesar so I won't be so dumb again?" I ask.

Both look at each other and nod.

"Okay Emmy, this could happen again. If you meet someone who is overly friendly or comes on fast romantically, stop as soon as possible and call it in. Then, stay with other friends you trust until we can check that person out. In other words, stay with who and what you know." Mom answers.

Dad adds, "Caesar is part of a group out of Italy that aided Germans out of Europe to South America. Your Mom and I have been making those hidden Germans uncomfortable and turned in those who are Nazis. We will be heading back to South America and Cuba after the holidays. So, we will be at it again. Be cautious."

I tell Mom and Dad that I am glad the boys are here in Washington .... All of the boys. Sean, Mike, Marty, Sterling and, of course, Charlie. I get up, hug and kiss Mom and Dad, and I excuse myself to bed. I have a lot to think about.

Sterling, Marty and Charlie are hoping for snow since these Texas boys did not grow up with a white Christmas. All are staying at our house. The day after Christmas we get snow, but we also get another surprise.

Carlos Ramos is coming to New York City with his new bride for their honeymoon. Our little team is immediately concerned. Did he have plans with Caesar or me, or is this really a honeymoon?

EIGHT

Langley OPS

- Carlos Ramos, his new wife, and two bodyguards arrive at JFK on December 28. They are staying at the Ritz Carlton and plan on staying two weeks. We'll need fingerprints on the entire party so we can tie them to crimes against American citizens.
- A team has been dispatched to retrieve the prints.
- Whitey, Big Bird, and their team have been apprised of their arrival.
- Tiger will be in Lexington Park for the New Year's Eve party. Naval Air Station Patuxent River will handle security.

NINE

The Invitation

AT FIRST, I'M NOT TOO concerned that Carlos will be in the country. That changes when a card arrives for me at the house. It's on nice stationery and looks like a wedding invitation. I have many friends getting married. As I turn it over to open, I'm startled by the return address. It says:

C.L.Ramos
The Ritz Carlton
50 Central Park South
New York City, NY 10019

I yelp, "What the hell?" and drop it.

People come from everywhere. Dad arrives first. I bend over to pick it up.

Charlie says, "Wait, it could have viable fingerprints. Did you open it?"

I answer, "No I didn't open it. I was just surprised that he knows where I am."

Everyone stops and waits. Sean steps up and takes over.

He says, "Charlie is right. No telling what is in that envelope. Sterling, call it in."

Sterling turns and heads for the phone. "Got it."

"Marty, we need a box or bowl to cover it until they arrive." Sean continues barking orders. "Charlie, take Kitten to the den, I will be there in a minute. Whitey and Big Bird, let's talk in here." They move into the formal living room.

I start to protest but Charlie moves me away before I can.

Sean stops and directs Sterling to stay with the letter. Marty brings a large Christmas box and covers the envelope where it fell.

Twenty minutes later, there's a team in the house picking up the envelope and taking it to the lab for evaluation. Sean, Mike and Dad leave with them. Sterling and Marty set about checking the security cameras and perimeter of the house and are working on night security. Mom, Charlie, and I sit in the den.

Mom asks me, "Tell me everything you can think of about Carlos."

Charlie said, "I'm recording so your Dad can hear this when he gets back, that way you only have to do this once. Then, we'll listen to it and see if anything is missing. Are you okay with that?"

Before I can answer, Mom says, "Charlie, I like how you think. Saving Emmy from doing this again and again is important."

"Okay, I agree to this, but will this ever end? Do you think Carlos is here to hurt me?"

Charlie was first to speak. "Emmy, don't worry right now. We'll find out what he is here to do. I think Langley really wants him connected to the other crimes so they will put manpower behind this investigation. That is why they need fingerprints and DNA."

"Emmy start from the beginning. When did you first meet him? I remember you said it was in Madrid," Mom said.

"Yes I did, but I didn't realize that until much later. He was helping all of us with our luggage from the airport to the motor coach. His friends were posing for pictures with us and he had the camera. I guess he was getting photos so he could sort us out."

Charlie sits up quickly and asks, "Do you still have that luggage?"

"Just the small carry-on," I answer.

"Is it here or in Houston?"

"It's here in my room."

Charlie is on the phone and asking for another team to pick up my carry-on immediately. He turns and as he hangs up, he and my Mom say together "tracker."

I've caught up, and I'm pissed now. "You think he put a tracker in or on my bag? How? When?"

Mom says to no one in particular, "It makes sense, that's how he found her in Houston."

"Yep, my thoughts exactly," Charlie answers.

This is crazy. Charlie asks me to continue with my story about Carlos because they'll need all the info they can get.

"Ok. I didn't meet him again in Salamanca until we were there about two weeks. Red was the one who introduced us. He made it sound like a dare, like I couldn't get along with the older teens. I resented his jabs at my maturity."

"Did Red hang out with you after he introduced you to Carlos?" Mom asked.

"Do you think Red could have been bribed to introduce you to Carlos?" Charlie asked.

"Mom, no, and Charlie, that is a tricky one. I hadn't thought about it like that, but Red and Scarlet always seemed flush with money and goodies. I don't think they're rich. I thought they put out, especially Scarlet."

Charlie stood and went to the phone. After a minute, he returned. "I called in a deep check on those two."

Mom shifted in her seat and asked, "Did Carlos try anything with you?"

I look Mom in the face and explain, "He kissed me once, but for me it was like kissing my brother or a cousin. I wasn't attracted to him, even though he is nice looking. Don't misunderstand, I liked him but I didn't LIKE him that way. He tried several times to get me to run away and marry him. He even said his dad knew about my dad and that he'd approve. And all of that in front of his fiancé! Weird, right?"

"Wait, he wanted to marry you?" Charlie almost shouted. I didn't even get time to answer before Mom asked "more importantly, he said his Dad knew about your Dad?"

Charlie blanched and said, "Oh yeah, that is telling. What did you tell him?"

I lean back and tell them both about the club and Carlos' asking me several times to go away with him and that he could keep me safe. I asked him, 'safe from what?' He never answered, he just smiled. He said he was better than Caesar. One time, Caesar threatened him and he left the club in a hurry. But not until he leaned in and told me I could have him any time. He even told me that the day I left that I could belong to him. I told him I belong to no one.

"He was there the morning you left? How did he know?" Mom started in immediately with questions. "Are you sure he was really engaged to the young girl in the club? I mean, was he affectionate? How old was she? Did she talk to you? Did you see a ring?"

I pause to think about her when the door opens. Dad, Sean, and Mike have arrived.

"Kitten, you have mail. It looks like it's from Eddie." Dad is talking and handing me letters as he approaches the sofa.

I am up and off the sofa examining the envelopes. I smile because he is right.

Mom says to all the guys, "Sit down and let's get this finished."

Dad hands me the envelope from earlier and some photos.

Sean comes close, points to the first photo and asks, "Who is Carlos and do you know the others?"

"Well, let's see.... This is Carlos and that's his younger brother. The other guy I don't know. Who's the girl? She's not the girl I met."

"Okay, just like we thought." Sean says, "The one you call Carlos is really Maximus, and Carlos is his younger brother. And the one you have not met is a hired gun. The girl pictured is Carlos' real bride of record."

"Perfect, lied to again. It never ends. Why did they lie? I just don't get it," I ask to no one and everyone.

Sean begins the explanation, "As we see it, the lie started with Red and Scarlet. Max used his brother's name when he slept with Scarlet and Red. He used his brother's name to hide in plain sight."

"What, wait? A threesome? He's bisexual? Why hide?"

"Well, Scarlet and Red talk a lot, and he is the oldest and most powerful so he was trying to stay in the shadows. Along came you, and he had to continue the ruse. He didn't need his play toys getting suspicious and he had promised them more fun once he got you softened up."

At that, I just couldn't contain myself. I jump up.

"Soften me up? What's that supposed to mean? If I could spend ten minutes with him I would…."

I stopped…. All eyes were staring at me.

"Ok, sorry. I'm just offended. Well, probably more than offended. More like angry with some violence attached." I smile and sit back down.

Everyone is trying not to laugh with me at my situation. With the tension released, not to mention a few laughs, I continue.

"Okay everyone, with that off my chest, what violence can I inflict on him while he is here? Bedbugs at the Ritz Carlton sounds good, for starters."

Sean is first to answer, "Well, Emmy, you can help if you want to."

Mom jumps up next. "I don't think so. She has been through enough."

Dad says, "Marie, can we talk? I think this idea has merit with minimal risk."

Now, I've heard my parents disagree but never has Dad had to ask us to leave the room and close the door to settle her down before. I look at the boys and almost in unison they shrug their shoulders and retreat to the kitchen. Not knowing what else to do, I follow them. As we arrive in the kitchen, I ask, "Do you think Dad needs help?

"NO!" All three speak as one.

Sean looks at me and says, "Whitey can handle your Mom. Big Bird gets her Mom on when it comes to you two. We know when to step back and let them work it out."

"How long?" I ask. Again, with the shoulder thing. "I am going upstairs if you need me. You know I will help."

TEN

Langley OPS

- New intel on Carlos Ramos. Kitten identified Maximus Ramos today as who she was led to belive was Carlos.
- The real Carlos is with Maximus and is who we've been watching as Caesar's partner, not Maximus.
- Our team has not yet been able to get close enough yet to get fingerprints. The only one who is likely to get close enough is Kitten.
- A second female arrived today with another bodyguard or brother. Passports suggest that they are related. Frank will get new photos to Sean so he can show them to Kitten. Sean will brief us on Whitey and Big Bird's thoughts on the plan.

ELEVEN

New Mission

Eddie's letters are safely stored under my mattress for now. I will read them again later and write him back. Reading them reminds me of how much I miss him. His letters this time talk about the country of Vietnam and not so much about the guys he is with. I'm glad that things there seem to be quiet where he is, for now. I wonder how long he has until he will be rotated out. I need to ask Dad.

Back in my room at home, it seems like it's been years since I have been here. There is a soft knock at the door. I start toward it, but stop. If I've learned anything, it's to be cautious about opening doors too quickly. I approach quietly and listen. Nothing, not a sound. Then, a soft knock and the question, "Did you watch Sesame Street....." I didn't wait for the rest of it. I opened it. Charlie stood there surprised.

"That's not the answer," he chided me.

"I know, but it was your voice. Besides, we are in my home with seven agents," I answer as I turn and walk to my bed.

"You're needed downstairs, things are developing as we speak. I'm your escort." Charlie went to the door, opened it and bowed. "M'lady your king and queen await your presence."

"Do you mean King Dad and Queen Mom?"

Charlie nods and I smile. As I start to parade past him, he grabs my elbow and pulls me into a kiss.... A good kiss and then bows again.

I make it downstairs and almost in the kitchen when I realize that there are a lot of people in the room. Many I know, several

I don't. Everyone is sitting at the table and all talking at once. I step in, and silence falls on the group. Heads swivel and all eyes are glued to me.

"What? I'm the elephant in the room, so at least throw me some peanuts." I smile and think that was a perfect intro.

Sean turns to Charlie and snarls, "Did you tell her?"

"No, I didn't tell her a thing, as ordered. She is just smart-mouthed like that, it runs in the family." As soon as his words left his mouth, he knew that he was in trouble. As I swiveled to let him have it, Mom beat me to it.

"Charlie, are you trying to hint that someone else is smart-mouthed in our little family?" she asks with a scary smile.

"No ma'am, I misspoke," Charlie answered quickly while simultaneously trying to disappear into the woodwork.

I knew I would have my time with him later.

Sean spoke next, bringing everyone back to the mission at hand. "Okay, most of you know everyone in the room, except for Kitten. I will help her, as we get to her part in this plan. Kitten has already said she will help, and her parents, Big Bird and Whitey, have approved with some strong suggestions."

Sean continues, "Kitten's exposure needs to be kept at a minimum. I know she will need to talk to Maximus, aka Carlos, but it will be in a public place. You all will still need to be on your toes."

"Please, don't make her Mom step in," Dad interjects.

"If that man gives me any cause, I will shoot him dead. So be there for my girl." Mom threatens the group.

I listen and want to ask questions, but not yet. It's time to just listen.

Sean seems to be leading the security detail with me, and Dad was leading the apprehension of subjects and collection of evidence. Sean looks at me and lays out my involvement. "We will need you place a call to Max, aka Carlos, to tell him that you can come to the wedding. You'll tell him that you would like to meet with him the day before for lunch at The Biltmore Hotel around 11:30 a.m. Let him know that, because of other things going on, you will have a chaperone with you but she will not be with you at the table. I will take care of security from there. Expect for him to change the time or the place that you suggest. Be agreeable. Give him your phone number. We are also aware he could change the location right up to the last moment. You will have alternatives as well, just not the Ritz. No worries, we will be listening."

I nod. "What number should I use? Will you be with me when he calls?"

"No, Charlie will. He is to stay at your side as much as possible, like in Houston. In New York City, we will add two local agents to assist. One will be with you, i.e. your chaperone, and the other will appear to be with Charlie, hiding in plain sight. Marty and Sterling will be close. Your Mom and Mike will be, we hope, in sniper position.

"Don't you think that I should ask Carlos, aka Max.... wait, no, I said that wrong.... This is crazy.... I get that the Carlos that I knew is really Maximus, so let's call him by his real name. Shouldn't I ask Maximus to bring everyone to lunch?" I ask.

Sean scrunches his eyebrows together. "Our surveillance on the group is that they usually lunch at the hotel. The only time they all leave is when the bride-to-be needs to see the seamstress about evening dresses she ordered, or a fitting for her wedding gown. We have secured that individual and will arrange a necessary fitting at the same time you are at lunch with Maximus. This should ensure the rooms are clear so that Whitey and his team can go in and secure DNA and fingerprints. We have a lot of details to iron out, but first we need to nail down the when and where."

"Ok, I'll do that now," I rise and head for the phone.

Sean says, "give me a moment, we need to set up, so we can hear. Emmy, if you call him Maximus, don't panic. Just tell him Caesar told you his real name. Try to keep the facade of your innocence as long as possible, it makes you feel like an easier target. If you forget, then be contrite and tell him you didn't mean to. He will enjoy an ego stroke. He's wanted your attention for a while so give it to him, shyly."

I stop dead, turn, and look at him straight in his beautiful eyes and say, "I've got this. I'm ready to make this happen, so we can finish this, permanently. How long until I can make the call?"

TWELVE

Langley OPS

- Whitey's detail is assigned to the hotel to collect prints and any intel there.
- Sean and Big Bird will lead the team with Kitten when she meets with Maximus Ramos.
- New York will add agents to help both teams.
- Ritz Carlton and seamstress are on board and ready to help with the surveillance of Max and his party.
- Tiger will remain in Lexington Park with her aunt.

THIRTEEN

New York

I HAVE ALWAYS LOVED NEW YORK with its constant movement and feeling so alive. Today, all the movement in the city makes me check over my shoulder. I know I am not alone, but I don't feel safe. I now know how dangerous Max, aka Carlos, really is, and I am entering his world willingly with eyes wide open. It is scary.

I can feel and sometimes see Charlie. My chaperone is Marilyn. She's nice and seems competent, as far as I can tell. The woman hanging on Charlie makes me feel weird, maybe even jealous. She is doing a good job of being the clingy girlfriend and Charlie is playing the part well. I don't see Mom, but that's a good thing, I think.

The restaurant at The Biltmore Hotel is just steps away and I can feel my heartbeat quicken. I'm warm all over. I don't see Max anywhere outside so I guess he got here first. As I step up to the hostess desk, I see him at a table far in the back. I wave and smile, then turn to Marilyn and say, "here goes nothing."

He stands and waits for me to make my way to him. I reach out to take his hand, and he pulls me in for a kiss. As he has me in his arms, I feel him feeling my back for a wire. Sean is so smart cause he said he would check. Sean said to act like I enjoy it, pretend it's Charlie so as to not give away my distaste for this closeness.

As I attempt to pretend Max is Charlie, he breaths in my hair and sighs against my neck. Then he steps in closer and says, "We are not alone." I push back and look at him as he releases me to my chair. This five-second kiss and embrace gives me pause. I am not sure if he sees everyone with me, or he is telling me that he came with someone. I smile and wait for him to sit. He checks out our surroundings one last time and sits. Our table is in the back and I can easily see the entrance and hostess. He can, too. Marilyn is not in sight and for that, I'm glad.

"So, my little kitten. I'm glad to see you and pleased that you will attend the wedding," Max says. I try not to show my alarm when he uses my call name. I'm certain he did that to throw me into a panic but, surprise, the boys had prepared me for that as well. The next thing he says does surprise me.

He continues with, "I am sorry Caesar was so rough with you. I thought he would honor my wishes when I told him to stand down but, as you know, he did not." My mind is confused. Is he telling me he did not orchestrate those encounters and has other plans for me? He goes on, "I know this invitation was last-minute. I would like to buy you a dress for the wedding and party that follows. My mother and father will arrive tonight to be here for the wedding and then go on to California to spend some time at one of the wineries. They return home to Spain in two weeks. I took the liberty of ordering lunch for you so we can save time, meet up with the others, and pick out a dress." I'm stunned, to say the least. I manage to nod. His smile is big and relieved, like he was afraid I would not go. I'm scared, but this is important and we will be in public. I am not alone.

"I made a reservation for you at the Ritz Carlton on our floor. Where is your luggage? Oh, and there is room in the suite for your chaperone, of course."

"Okay. What am I having for lunch?" I ask, just as big plates with a hamburger and french fries arrive for each of us.

He smiles and says, "It's a typical American lunch, right?"

I smile, nod and take a bite of my burger so I don't have to talk. He seems more than willing to talk, so I let him.

"Where are your parents? Are they here or out of the country?" he asks.

I have been eating while he talks and I almost choke. For a moment, I think he's on to me. His next sentence makes me realize he is just trying to make small talk with me.

"I'm surprised your mother or father is not with you, so I figured they must be away. It is Christmas and I thought that they might be here during this time."

I look at him and decide to stick to as much of the truth as I can. I answer him with, "Mom and Dad are still in the country, but I am not sure exactly where they are just this minute. Marilyn is someone Mom has known for a while. She is nice but can be a pain sometimes."

We are silent for a moment as we both get lost in our lunch. I am brought back to reality, as I hear a gasp. As I look towards the hostess, I experience joy and turmoil at once. My eyes see, but don't register, the hostess leading Eddie, my Eddie, and a small woman trailing behind him. Max sees my confusion and smiles triumphantly. Eddie sees me, turns, and nods to the woman who has been seated a couple of tables away. She is pregnant, and she kisses him on the cheek as he releases her hand. It is a loving kiss, not a sibling kiss, and her look at me is sad.

Eddie comes straight for me. Max stands and greets Eddie, and it's then that I know I've been set up for this pain. My brain is freaking out. What is going on? I feel sick. I want to disappear. I want to kill Max, because he did this. Eddie did this, too. Has he changed so much that he would embarrass me in person?

Eddie is angry and sad all in one. His words for me are, "I didn't know you would be here. This is not how I wanted to have this conversation."

I don't know how I managed to speak, not shout, cry or strike him, but I did. "Even a letter would have been better than this. To allow me to be hurt in public, I guess you have changed. I love a different Eddie," I sputtered out quietly.

Eddie glares at Max and tries to take my hands, but I step back. Eddie speaks and I think he is holding back tears. "I deserve your anger. I would like to explain, but this is not the time nor place. I hope you will give me that chance. "

I look over his shoulder and ask, "Yours?"

He nods, not needing clarification on my question of paternity, and while I take off the necklace with his ring on it, I push on. "I think you may need this, or at least the money you can get for it. Please walk away before one of us says more than is needed. I would like to keep my dignity. As for your explanation, I can't say that will make much of a difference seeing as how she is carrying your child. Do the Millers know?" He nods. "Well, that takes the cake. I am the last to know and I should have been the first. Goodbye, Eddie."

I sit. I am sick to my stomach and want to puke. I can't finish my burger or anything else. Max leaves the table and follows Eddie out of the dining area, along with the small, Asian girl. I can hear angry words from both men, then silence. Max returns to the table and sits. He says, "I'm sorry, you needed to know what kind of man you were waiting on. Whenever you're done, we should go."

I let my napkin fall to the floor and quickly pick it up again. It's the signal that I'm going with him. I'm numb. I know that this is important, even though I want to run and hide. I look at Max and say, "I'm ready, but I must take Marilyn with me." He nods, stands and extends his hand to help me up and into his arms again. He wants to embrace, but that is not happening.

I read his face. He seems to be enthralled and almost unable to believe I'm still going with him. Of course, in my head, this is a mission and not at all what I would want. This is weird. He has just publicly taken a dream from me and he thinks I want to be in his arms? What a creep!

FOURTEEN

Langley OPS

- A report from Sean in New York has revealed that Max used Eddie Lysinger to hurt and shock Kitten in the restaurant. Big Bird came close to taking him down herself, but Kitten signaled all was well and that kept the mission viable. Tough girl, like her Mom.
- New York team is following Lysinger until they get word from us. Big Bird wants to question him. We have ordered him brought in, unharmed.

FIFTEEN

The Dress

THE DRESSMAKER IS NOT FAR from the restaurant so we walk the three blocks. After introductions, Marilyn excuses herself to the bookstore next door to the dressmaker. I'm still numb and she's aware. I've locked down my head just to keep going. I know Sean already has security here at the dressmakers. I don't drink, but I really need to get drunk and disappear. Just not until I get this jackass holding my hand in jail.

As we enter, the real Carlos greets us with, "Hey Max, I'm glad you convinced her to come." Max had me by the hand and I felt him stiffen with the mention of his real name out loud. He stops dead, turns to me and leans in close. He softly breaths in my ear, "My name is Max, not Carlos. I am sorry for the lie. At the time we met, it could not be avoided. Please don't judge me too harshly."

I want to say, "Oh, you mean you don't want me strung blindly along as one of your playthings?" Instead I say, "I already knew. Caesar told me, but I didn't want to embarrass or hurt you."

He smiles, kisses me on the cheek, and says to the room, "Let's get this dress out of the way. I have other things to do while Emmy is in town. I think she would look stunning in blue, a deep blue like her eyes."

I really don't care what color or style of dress at this point, but when she brings out a rack of dresses that I wouldn't even look at, much less wear, I begin to take notice. Each dress looked like I would need to be greased up to slide into. None of them would allow for any undergarments or leave anything to the imagination. So sick.

Okay. I hope I don't have to actually wear this, but here I go. I am alone in the dressing room for a few minutes and I need to regroup in my head. I am just about to come out and parade around in the first of six dresses for Max's approval when a small girl comes in to help me into the dress. I am already in it, but she has a paper cup with water, which she offers to me. I refuse, but she insists. I take it and as I go to take a sip, there on the bottom are letters. It says, "R U OK? ~C" I look up in surprise, she smiles, and I nod. She motions to me to drink it and I do. She flattens the inside cup and puts it inside her waistband. She hands me the empty outer cup and points to the trash can. I put it to my mouth and throw it in the can as I open the door.

Max watches me and says, "You look like you need something stronger than water."

I answer, "Nope, that was exactly what I needed." It really is what I need. I need to know Charlie is out there and has my back.

Three dresses later, Max has found the dress he thinks is perfect, so I go along with it, too. The new dress will be delivered to the hotel. I feel like shit and I see no hope at feeling better in the near future.

SIXTEEN

Langley OPS

- Lysinger has lost his tail. Get on that.
- Fingerprints and intel confirm Max and male parties in his group are all part of the attempts on Kitten and Karly in the past.
- Arrest warrants are in the works. Big Bird and Whitey will escort them back to Washington for interrogations.

SEVENTEEN

Carlton Ritz

A CAR IS WAITING AT THE curb when we emerge from the dressmaker. As I get in, I think I see Charlie across the street in a cafe window. He is embracing a girl and looking over her shoulder. I want to be that girl.

The Carlton Ritz is beautiful and I wish I could enjoy this luxury. Max has me by the arm. It's not a loving grip. He is holding me so tight, I know I will have bruises where his fingers are. I feel like a prisoner. The hotel lobby is busy, but as we approach the elevators I see Eddie, again. He is alone. He is coming toward me again. I want alone time with him, and I don't. Max has me by the elbow and he is pulling me back to him. I shake loose and say, "Max, you put me in this situation. At least let me end this with some dignity." He nods and steps back.

Eddie points to a small alcove to my left. I head there and turn to look him in the eye. I can see he has been crying and his voice is shaky when he speaks. "I still love you, and I always will, but I have a duty to the life I've made. I hope you will forgive me someday." I thought I could talk to him, but I couldn't. My heart was wailing inside me. My knees are weak. My stomach was rolling around. But I just stand still and let pain run down my face. He pulls a handkerchief from his pocket and tries to wipe the tears away. I let him.

"You need time to work this out, don't you? I've missed you and I will miss you forever," he says. He pulled me into him. I could see Max start towards me. I shook my head no and he stops. I could not help myself, I returned Eddie's embrace. I will never have this again. He whispers in my ear, "Thank you for this. I will cherish it forever."

I whisper back to him, "Max is a bad man. Get out of this hotel and run far away." Eddie leans back and grabs me tighter again. He says. "I know that now, but...."

I interrupt him and say, "Goodbye, my love. It's time to turn and leave in the opposite direction of Max. Do it now. I'm going to slap you so he thinks I hate you. That might save you. If he thinks you are no threat, he might not kill you. Get ready and go." I push back and slap him. I don't know how I thought I would feel, but I turn and throw up. Max rushes forward and catches me as I slide down to the floor. Thank goodness Eddie is gone when I look back. I do my best to keep Max and his man engaged with my needs while I try to give Eddie time to escape Max.

Max and company, with Marilyn in tow, get me to the suite. My luggage is there. Max tells Marilyn he will be back. I go straight to the bathroom. I strip out of my clothes and step into the shower. I cry. Thirty minutes or so when I come back out, all was quiet. I am glad I do not have to talk to anyone. I climb into bed and fall asleep before my head hits the pillow.

EIGHTEEN

Langley OPS

- Lysinger was taken into protective custody along with his pregnant wife. They will be transported to Washington separate from the others.
- Max and company were arrested without incident and are en route as we speak.
- Whitey and Big Bird are on their way, too.
- Charlie and Sterling will escort Kitten back as soon as she is fit to travel.
- Sean and Marty, with the help of the New York team, will clean up in New York and be here in two days.

NINETEEN

Moving On

Marilyn is not around when I wake up, which worries me. I order food and soon it arrives. At the knock at the door, I look through the peephole. Relief rushes through me. It's not Max or one of his goons. Any one out there was better than Max and company. The room service attendant has a hat on and is looking down at the door handle so I can not clearly see him but I am sure it is not Max or someone from his group. I open it and let the room service attendant in. As he pushes the cart past me, I hear Sean and Charlie in my head, scolding me about being too quick to open doors. Too late, he's already in.

I'm get really worried when the room service guy grabs me by the arm. Oh God, do I have to fight for my life again? He pulls me in close and I'm ready to headbutt him when I see Charlie's smile.

He kisses me and says, "It's over, you're done. You only have to escape me." I hold him tight, then release him and wonder if he knows about Eddie. Of course he does. Did he know before it happened? He puts both hands on my face and comes in close and says, "We need to talk and no one will bother you until tomorrow, as soon as I radio in and say you are safe and asleep." He steps aside and talks quickly into his radio, "All is well. I'll take night duty."

He pats the metal domes. "Your next choice, after you eat, is where we should talk. I have my preference, but you're the boss on this one." I smile and sit down to eat. I'm starved.

"Is it really over?" are my first words after a couple of bites. He nods. "Where is Marilyn?" I ask.

He smiles a sneaky smile and replies, "I asked if I could break the news and trade places on the security detail. Your parents are on their way back to Washington, with the prisoners in tow. We will go there in the morning. Are you okay?"

I smile back, nod and continue eating. We sit in thoughtful silence as I finish eating. Charlie looks at me and says, "Should we talk here on the sofa or there in the bedroom?" I want him to hold me and I want the pain I feel at Eddie's betrayal to be gone. For now, I'll take the arms of Charlie. Mentally, I choose the bedroom. If we manage to talk, good, but if we don't, I'm okay with that, too. I need his warmth and the safety of his presence. The guilt of my promise to Eddie is gone and I want to devour Charlie now that I can with a clear conscience. He's still waiting for an answer.

I stand and turn for the bedroom. I look over my shoulder, drop the robe I have on and head for the bed. He has a full view of a naked me wanting him. I hear the door double locked. Charlie is quick to follow, disrobing as he follows. We've slept together, but never been intimate. He knows how I feel about being a virgin when I get married. Today, I just don't know how I feel about that anymore.

He climbs in and I'm dazzled by his body. Not only is he beautiful, but parts of him are ready and bigger than I expected. I am staring. He says, "Is something wrong?"

I stammer but finally find my voice. "No, on the contrary, you are more than I expected and I think I love it."

He chuckles and moves closer. "It works well, too." I blush.

Charlie uses his hands to explore me and sighs into my hair. I feel him move and get harder. He whispers, "I have dreamed of this moment. You are everything a man could want and this man has wanted you." I can't help but melt into him. He continues, "I need to know your rules tonight so I don't spoil a good thing by hurting you. I can wait, even if it will be the hardest thing I've ever done."

"My rules are changing by the minute. I want you and I am not sure why I've waited. I don't have protection, do you? I'm not afraid to have sex with you. I'm nervous and worried that I don't know enough to please you."

Charlie hushes me with his finger gently across my lips. "Let's play it by ear. Yes, I have protection. I've wanted this for so long. I need to touch you all over and breathe you in. So, let's enjoy the moment." With that, we did. I discovered that I really like sex with Charlie. We might need to do this all the time.

In the morning, I ask Charlie a silly question. Well, it's not silly to me but, due to my lack of experience, I need to ask. I have heard that once you've had sex, it's obvious and others can tell. I ask him how that works. He grabs me, pulls me close and laughs. "I'm serious!" I shout.

He says, "Sorry, I guess some people can tell, or guess, if they really know you. Just don't get sensitive and admit to anything. I won't."

"Are you sure?" I insist. Charlie just kisses me and says it's time to go.

TWENTY

Langley OPS

- Check your assigned teams to interrogate all of Max's group.
- Big Bird and Whitey will be listening and watching.
- Kitten should arrive today and will be in Georgetown home with Charlie and Sterling.
- Tiger is still in Lexington Park at her aunt's until January 2.

TWENTY-ONE

Healing Again

THE CAR IS WAITING FOR the five-hour drive home. Charlie and I do talk about Eddie and what he knows. It seems Max befriended him and arranged for him and his new bride to be in that restaurant at the same time I was.

"Max thought it would show you that he was loyal and Eddie was not. Eddie had called the Millers to find out where you were, and planned to find you and explain." Charlie said he was in the lobby and had been the one to take Eddie to Mom after I slapped him.

"Eddie told your mom that while in Vietnam, he got separated from his patrol and was hidden by her family for three months. He was wounded and she nursed him back to health. Eddie thought he was a dead man. Over time and in their closeness, things happened. He eventually was reunited with his company, only to discover that he was the only one who survived from his patrol.

"Eddie is one messed up man. He relives that nightmare every night when he closes his eyes. He does not seem to be the man you described to me. He seems haunted. He didn't know she was pregnant until a few weeks before he was scheduled to come home. He said he was raised to be a responsible man, and to leave his baby behind was something he could not do.

"The U.S. government would not let him bring her here to have his son without marrying her. He made that choice for his son. He hopes he can be a good dad, and maybe learn to love her as a wife, not just for her kindness when he was wounded.

Your dad is getting him help with the demons that are in his head. Your dad said he owed him that. Had there not been a baby depending on him, I think suicide would not be out of the question.

"He needs a lot of professional help. He told your mom he had already decided to break things off with you when he found out he was a father. He knows you deserve more than what he has to offer right now."

All of this is hard to hear. It makes me want to help him and I tell Charlie that.

Charlie answers, "Your mom and dad said that you would feel that way. Eddie said as much, too. The Millers already have a job for him and a place for him to live and try to work things out in his head. Your dad found psychiatric care specializing in PTSD close to the Millers for him. Eddie wants to know what to do to make you move on and not look back. Max might have jumped the gun, but he couldn't lie to you and that is why he came back to the hotel. He hopes you'll wait ten years to check on him and reconnect and meet his son. Your mom and dad said that they could not promise that but would suggest it to you."

My head and heart are about to explode. I close my eyes and Charlie pulls me close and says, "Think, sleep and dream. You will know what to do after that. I just want to be a part of it." I smile, cuddle close and whisper, "You will. I love you." I felt him hold me tighter just as I fell asleep.

TWENTY-TWO

Langley OPS

- Prosecution of all of the subjects will begin in three months. All intel and evidence needs to be on my desk ASAP for transport to the prosecutor's office.
- Big Bird and Whitey will leave after Tiger is settled in school for the new year.
- Kitten is heading back to school in Houston. Her team will be reduced now that we have the subjects behind bars.
- Carlos and Max's parents' visas have been revoked indefinitely.
- Charlie, Marty and Sterling of the Houston team will decide how much surveillance Kitten needs.

TWENTY-THREE

A New Beginning

A NEW BEGINNING FOR ME HAD always included Eddie. My heart still has a hole in it, but Tootsie says that Eddie is sick, and she misses the old Eddie. There are glimmers now and again of his old self that gives her hope. Tootsie says Eddie's wife is as shy as a small bird, and that he clearly respects her, but is constantly worrying about their baby on the way.

I asked Tootsie if he mentions me. "Emmy, when he saw the picture of you and him hanging on the wall in the den, he smiled and said that is from another life. The one he lost in Vietnam." This made my eyes well up with tears. I also asked her if I should be there to help him. I feel it is my duty.

She said, "It would be easy to tell you to come, but that would be more for my sake and not Eddie's. He's moving forward slowly, and his unborn son is his connection to his life to come. You might make him lose his very light grasp on stability. Bob is so very good with him, so no, you should finish school and learn be you, without him."

My new beginning is in good ole Houston. I don't get to keep the apartment that I lived in. It was cozy and there were so many great memories with Charlie there. A friend of mine that I met through my sorority sisters has invited me to stay with him in his two-bedroom apartment until a safe alternative can be found. Jim Morris, a law student who used to date one of my sisters, is who I'm rooming with temporarily. We've always gotten along from the beginning. He works part-time as a private detective, which he says will help him in the future since he plans to be a lawyer. Charlie doesn't like this much, but for now it will have to do. When I first get back, Charlie and Sterling receive assignments that take them out of state for a month. Marty is my man during that time. He and I have an understanding that if I am not with Jim, I'm to call him in. My classes are scheduled tight on Monday, Wednesday and Friday. Tuesday and Thursday just have one morning class. Marty attends class with me. He especially likes my human sexuality class and my sorority sisters, go figure.

Jim's cute and I find him attractive, as do many girls. He can have his pick, and pick he does. There is a parade in and out of his bedroom. It's a little annoying, trying to dodge them at night so I don't cramp his style, heaven forbid. Sometimes, he asks me to help with an investigation. He says I'm good at talking to people I don't know. I can get them to talk. When I talk to strangers, it drives Charlie crazy because they can't tell Jim's bad guys from real bad guys. Jim thinks his concern about 'bad guys' is funny. While Charlie is out of town, Jim becomes possessive. Jim just doesn't know the full story about me or my past life. I feel it's better that way.

School is a cross between normal and the paranormal. Class assignments are easy, but it's my sorority sisters that seem to lean more toward the Twilight Zone. I can't believe how different each one is. You would think that like-minded girls would be in a sorority together, but that is not the case. For example, there is Kaye, a beauty queen and preacher's daughter, who is wound up so tight that I think she might explode if someone curses in front of her. Contrast that with me and my baggage of weirdness.

Jim and I are at the apartment and it's the second week that Charlie has been gone on assignment. Completely out of the blue, Jim asks me, "Are you having sex with just Charlie, or the other guys, too?"

I'm stunned silent. Jim and I have talked on tons of subjects, including sex, but never on details like who, when and why. It took me a minute, and then I answered, "If that were any of your business, I might answer, but it's not. Why did you ask that, and do you really expect a straight answer?"

Jim smiles and says, "I want to know because I want to know.

I just needed to know if there is room for me." I laugh, thinking he's kidding, but he moves closer to me on the sofa. "So, what's your answer? God, I hope it's all cause then I know there's room for me."

I laugh again. He's serious, but I'm not frightened by Jim. He is attractive, there is no chance for sex. I really like Charlie and even though we have not made a verbal commitment of exclusivity, I kind of feel we have.

Jim noticed that I'm not going to answer him. He hops up and says, "You want a drink? We have work to do on the new assignment and I need your help." The tense moment has passed.

Jim brings back a Sprite. He says he is out and asks if Sprite will do. I nod and take a sip, even though I really only like Coke. I start munching on a cookie, one of his special chocolate chip ones, and before I know it, I've eaten four.

We finish our surveillance plan for the next day and sit back to watch a little TV. Jim has a video recorded and pops in a film he wants me to watch and tell him my opinion of it. I like looking at his surveillance films for clues.

I feel alive and content, and I like movies, so this seems to be an easy way to help him. I'm in shorts and a t-shirt, and so is Jim, but it starts to feel hot in the apartment so I adjust the temperature of the AC. The video starts on a party, but soon everyone is taking off their clothes.

I look at Jim and he's watching me. "Jim, is this one of your surveillance recordings?"

I'm intrigued. I've never seen a movie where people take their clothes off and walk around nude, showing everything. Soon, they're kissing and not just on the lips. I'm hypnotized and can't take my eyes off the screen. I'm afraid to look at Jim. I don't want to look like I am new to this kind of nudity and sexual behavior, even though I am. I'm becoming aroused and start to want what is happening on the screen.

I tell Jim I'm hungry. Jim smirks and leaves the room for the kitchen.

He calls from the kitchen, "Will chocolate ice cream be okay?"
I answer, "Yes, sounds delicious."
"I have whipped cream too," he calls out.

"I like it all, I'm just hungry," I answer. He chuckles at my answer.

The last time I felt this hungry without reason was back when I was at Woodstock and we had been wandering through so many folks smoking weed. There's a clue.

While he's gone, I decide to remove my bra so I won't be so warm. I put my t-shirt back on and realize my nipples are erect even though I'm so warm. Being excited by the movie is a new experience for me. Everything on the screen teeters between sexy or funny.

Jim returns from the kitchen with a large bowl of ice cream in front of him, a plate of whipped cream, and nothing else. What I mean is, he's stark naked and holding the bowl in one hand, and the plate low with his manhood is laying under the whipped cream with a cherry on top in the other. He announces, "I'm hot and trying to cool off. Since you've made me so hot, it's your responsibility to fix that because this whipped cream isn't doing the trick. Get over here, goddess, and fix this mess."

Jim is funny like that and I'm giggling when he sets the ice cream, but not the plate, on the coffee table and joins me on the sofa. He scoots next to me, plate in lap, and pulls my shirt off. At this point, whipped cream is everywhere, but I don't care. His face is buried in my breasts and he begins to suck on a nipple. I find it's a big turn on for me and I want more. I have never even thought of having sex with him, but he clearly has with me. He says so as he undresses me further, pulling off my shorts and panties. He is smooth and practiced at this. After some more whipped cream messiness and attention to my breasts, he stands me up on my feet, yanks me over his shoulder, and walks to his bedroom, slapping my behind as he goes.

In the morning, I know we had sex and it was naughty, but I don't remember much beyond that. Right now, my head hurts. Somehow, I'm in my own bed. What have I done? But really, the question is, why had I done it? At the time it felt right, but now not so much. I hate how I feel about this, it's so confusing. I shouldn't have let that happen. My head hurts and I need an aspirin.

As I'm searching for some relief in the kitchen, I ponder

on what to say and how to act around Jim. He solves that. He says, "Sex with you last night was great. We were both so high, though, that I'd like to do that again sober and see what we think."

I turn and explode at him. "You got me high? How..." I stop mid-thought and realize the Sprite must have had something in it.

He smiles a sheepish smile and says, "I thought you knew my cookies had weed in them and the Sprite had alcohol in it, lots of it."

Crap... I'm so stupid. "Jim, I don't drink, at all. I didn't recognize the alcohol taste. As for the cookies, I thought they were just expensive and, in the past, you just didn't like to share."

He grins, reaches for me and says, "they are expensive and you were worth it. Was I? I want to try you on again."

I break out of his grip on my elbows. "Jim, I trusted you! I've only had sex with one other man. How could you? You should have asked. I didn't say yes." I shouted.

"You did say yes when you watched the porno, had the drink and ate the cookies. That was a green light to me," he calmly answers.

I don't know what to say. Is that consent? I decide it's not in my dictionary. I turn and storm to my room to think. I did like it, at least what I remember. It was different than with Charlie. It was not just plain naughty, but also physically satisfying.

What is love, what is lust, and who am I in this picture? I need answers. I really don't have anyone to talk to about this. Caroline is gone, Tootsie would not understand and my mom would just want to kill someone. I need out of here before Jim gets it in his head to try again.

It's Tuesday and Marty will be here soon so I need to hustle to get ready. I feel icky, so in the shower I scrub better than I ever have before. I get dressed and leave hoping that Marty is here early. Marty has made it known that he is attracted to me, but he respects my wishes not to be pushy or take initiative. Why didn't Jim? Marty has a model quality that the others don't. He is perceptive and it feels sometimes like he reads my mind. Today would be a good day for me to conceal my thoughts. I don't know if I should share with him about how stupid I've been.

I'm ready and out the door before Jim can corner me about having sex again. I will have to do something about that soon.

Marty is sitting in his car when I come out. He looks up as I get in the car, smiles big and says,"I just love going to your Human Sexuality class. The only thing is, it gets me aroused. I hope to see some of your sisters so maybe I can share that arousal with them." I just stare at him, silent, even though I am wondering if all men think of sex all the time. Marty waves a hand in front of my face. "Hey kid, are you there? Where's the girl who chastises me for talking about my sexual appetite?"

I only hear the words 'kid' and 'girl', and want to show him how far off he is. I reach over and grab the front of his shirt and plant a stellar kiss on him. I pull back from a surprised man and sort of shout, "I am not child... Was that proof enough, or do you need more?"

Marty just sits there with his mouth open for a moment, but then regains some composure. "I would love more, but Charlie is my best friend and I respect you. What's going on that brought you to the 'I am woman, hear me roar' point of showing me you're a full-fledged, sexual woman? Cause I already knew that," Marty asks.

I stiffen, but then just drop back in the seat and fall apart. "I don't know what to do or what I want. No, I want Charlie here. I need him in my arms. Marty, you're great. And, well, Jim is… but I won't be able to keep dodging him. And Jim only just recently became an issue since I was drunk or drugged, well really both. Oh God, I'm so mad at myself." I drop my head in my hands and wonder when I became this wishy-washy and out of control.

There was some silence, peppered with some clearly measured breathing and then, "You were drugged? Are you telling me that Jim got you drunk, and then gave you drugs, and then had sex with you?" Marty's voice rises with each word as he sort-of whispers loudly, holding back a hidden crazy man inside.

I nod and burst into tears. Marty moves in close and holds me. I am slobbering into his shoulder as he declares, "I will kill him... No, torture... No, just torment him until Charlie gets home. Charlie will do the killing."

I try to compose myself enough to get Marty to back up a little. I lean away enough to look into his beautiful eyes and say, "I am so sorry I kissed you."

"I'm not. It was delicious and I'd welcome more but Charlie is my best friend so you're off-limits," he answers back.

"I was a willing participant last night, even though I was drunk and drugged. The marijuana cookies made me compliant, and willing, so it is partly my fault. I just don't know how to make him understand that I am not interested in doing that again, sober or not." I can see Marty's patience straining.

"That kind of sex is not consensual. You did not come after him. It is not your fault, so stop blaming yourself. How old is he? You're just eighteen and he is twenty-something, right? Two or three years' difference when you reach your forties is no big deal, but at eighteen? That's a giant difference. A case could be made for rape," Marty says in measured words.

I reach out and put my hand on his. I am not sure what to say. I really am confused and angry at myself and the whole situation. I look up, deciding he can help just by listening.

"Marty, I need a friend that isn't going to try to take me to bed. I know I'm emotionally immature, but I need guidance or at least your opinion and advice. Charlie and I have been through a lot together. He is my angel, I'm attracted to him and might even love him. Have I ruined things by sleeping with him before we decide that this is forever? I mean, in Catholic schools you are taught to wait until marriage. If he is not the one, or he finds someone else, will anyone else want someone like me? God, this is embarrassing, telling you this, You're an attractive, sexy man that I would jump at if I wasn't so into Charlie. Would you even look at me knowing what you know?"

Marty leans in, kisses me on the forehead and says, "I would have you any chance I had. It's not branded on your forehead that you've had sex with anyone. Any real man wouldn't care. I don't care. I don't think Charlie and I will be able to let Jim think that it's okay to take advantage of you. I will always be your friend and you can tell me anything, except state secrets."

It takes me a minute and I whisper, "Thank you for listening and caring." As I say this, I can tell Marty conflicting feelings about Jim reach a boiling point. I can tell he is rethinking waiting for Charlie. I put my hand on his, hoping to calm him. It doesn't' work.

Marty explodes, "Is he in there right now? I can make him understand. It will only take a minute. It's the least I can do."

He looks like he's about to jump out of the car. His anger would make things worse. I put my arms around him and say, "Can we get something to eat? I'm starving and have a hangover, so I think food might help. Maiming Jim can wait until after breakfast."

He looks at me for a minute. I can see him change and settle.

"Yes, princess," Marty says through gritted teeth as he puts the car in gear. Food does help and I feel better. I can see on his face, and hear in his voice, that Marty is ready for action that involves Jim and his fist.

I'm worried about things like Jim coming to my room when I'm asleep and climbing in for a repeat adventure. Marty must be reading my mind because he leans across the table and tells me I have three choices. "One: I can kill Jim, so problem solved. I'm only half-joking about that. Two: I can come and sleep in your room, or three: you can come and stay at my place. Your choice. Decide, soon."

"I think you invading his space is not good. It is his home and my place will be available in two weeks. If you have room, I think your place is the better idea. Do you think we will be creating a bigger problem with Charlie if I do that?" I answer.

Marty smiles a sneaky smile and says, "Let me handle telling Charlie about the address change. He'll be home just in time to move you to your new place. He can reclaim his territory then. I think ultimately he'll be grateful that I took you away from that environment."

I sit there thinking about how to inform my parents and my friends. It looks like I'm moving from one man's place to another. That is not so good for a girl's reputation. Marty interrupts my thoughts with, "Kitten, you're deep in thought. What's up?"

I sigh, smile and explain how I feel about my reputation.

"Charlie will understand and your parents trust you, and us, to keep you safe. Your girlfriends will be jealous, especially since you will be at my place. As for the guys, they'll probably wonder why it's not them." Marty proudly states. "Let's get to class. We can't miss Human Sexuality. We might need the info imparted today for tonight."

Jim isn't home when I vacate his apartment. I'll see him tonight because I promised to help him with one of his assignments. We will be watching some guy while he is out and about. Jim needs pictures of him being unfaithful. I'm to be his cover, so I'll tell him then. Not so fun, but necessary. I can't trust Marty with him. I know Marty will be watching so no worries, at least not from Jim.

Marty takes me to the meet-up. Jim is waiting. I can tell Jim hasn't been home because he doesn't say anything about my stuff being gone.

Jim looks at Marty and says. "I got this. She's safe with me."

That was the trigger that sets Marty off. He steps up close, grabs Jim by his shirt, and lifts him up and out of his seat.

Marty says between clenched teeth, "Don't you ever put a hand on Emmy again or I will make you regret it. I'm restraining myself, for now. Even though you're a huge dickhead, she insisted on being here to help you. Give me a reason to change my mind about taking you out."

Jim immediately spit out, "What? She wanted it. She took her bra off and laid down on the sofa and watched the porn movie, happily. I don't see what the problem is."

Ninja-like reflexes landed Jim with a bloody nose and badly bruised balls before he saw it coming. "There's a sample. She is not interested in you. Stay. Away," Marty spits out.

"Kinda hard to do that seeing as how she lives with me," Jim spits right back.

"That mistake has been fixed so eat your own ice cream."

Jim's head whips around to me. He scowls at me like I've divulged a state secret. Well, his state secret. I get the feeling that the ice cream routine was just that, a routine.

I step around Marty and say, "I know this is important tonight, so let's go, bloody nose and all. I know what to do. I will get a table where you said was best." I'm across the street before either man can speak.

The hostess at the restaurant takes me to the perfect table. I know Jim will approve.

Even though Marty has given Jim a sampling of what will come his way if he's not careful, Jim acts like everything is normal. The evening is progressing along as expected, the mark arrives with a knock-out on his arm and Jim photographs everything.

I know the info on the man in question. He is a forty-year-old married man with two kids. The surprise is who he's brought to dinner. I know her. She's a transfer student from Dallas and a sorority sister. I don't know her well, but I do know she's the newly crowned Miss Southwest Conference. She notices me. Marty is close by and watching everything.

Kaye smiles and waves. I wave back. She leans in to speak to the mark and then gets up and comes over. As she approaches, Jim leans in close and says, "Do you know her?"

I nod. Jim freaks out. "What the hell?"

I glare at Jim and whisper, "How was I to know your perv is taking out one of my sorority sisters?"

I turn and say, "Hi Kaye. What brings you here?"

Kaye smiles big and explains as she helps herself to the chair next to me. "He's this old married dude that likes sweet young things. I guess the term is a 'Sugar Daddy'. I like all the money he spends on me and he needs so little entertainment at his age."

Jim huffs, "What kind of entertainment?"

Kaye cuts her eyes his way, as if she just remembered he's there. "You'll have to pay to find that out and I am too expensive for the likes of you." I snicker because it's so true.

"How much does it cost to talk to you in private?" I can't believe I hear what sounds like genuine interest. Kaye winks, writes her number on the napkin and pushes it towards Jim.

"Emmy, you should have told me we have something in common. Maybe I've underestimated your bank roll, Jim. It is Jim, right? And just so you know, I sometimes enjoy the company of more than one at a time, just not sure if Emmy is into that." Kaye is up and gone before I can say a word.

Jim is waving at the waitress for the bill. "We can leave,

Emmy. I got what I wanted and more." He pauses, then smiles and looks me straight in the face. "Are you into a threesome? I could be talked into that."

I calmly look back at him, but underneath the table I lift my foot, place it on the chair between his legs and kick. The chair goes flying back, landing Jim on his back on the floor. During his descent, Jim caught the table cloth, rather than the table, on his way back to the floor, littering him with dishes and uneaten food. Everyone in the restaurant turns and gawks. I am up and walking away before he even hits the floor, never even looking back. The commotion behind me is satisfying enough. I hear glass breaking, women gasping, and I envision a seriously pissed off man. I hope he is wearing every saucy piece of food from the table. Tomato sauce stains. I send a mental 'thank you' to the cook at this lovely Italian restaurant for that. It will just accentuate his sliminess. Such power, I love it. I feel like superwoman.

Marty is by my side as I get to the door. "Are you alright? Can I go back and kill him?"

I cut my eyes at him. "I'm better than ever, let's get out of here."

Marty and I hop into his car and drive off. I look in the side mirror to see Jim at the curb, really unhappy. "You know Marty, that felt good to put him in his place. Maybe Jim will think twice about taking advantage of other girls." Marty didn't even look at me, he just stared ahead. "Emmy, men like him never learn. He will do it again and again, until he crosses the line and gets seriously hurt or goes jail."

TWENTY-FOUR

Houston OPS

- Kitten is being moved to a new location for two weeks until a permanent location is ready.
- Parents are still out of country.

TWENTY-FIVE

Marty

———

MARTY'S PLACE IS NOT WHAT I expect. I guess I expected something like Jim's place, all leather and dark. To my surprise, his place is light, airy and really just beautiful. It's in a high rise in the Galleria area and has an amazing view of downtown. The living room and kitchen are mostly light grey and stainless steel. The accent color is orange, which I would not have guessed. Not Halloween orange but UT orange, burnt orange.

As you walk in, you're drawn to the large wall of windows and the view. The sofa and loveseat make an L, allowing you to see it all. The windows are floor to ceiling and it makes the burnt orange sofa and loveseat seem to float in the space of all the grey, from the luxurious rug to the soft grey walls and tile. When I sit on the sofa, I feel like I'm floating in a cloud.

Marty shows me where I will be sleeping, a loft above the living room. I sit on the bed and I can still see the view, even though there's a glass wall that separates the two spaces. There are drapes across the glass that close for privacy but I know that at night I plan to open them so I can look out at the lights of the city. My room has a beautiful bathroom attached. I have everything a girl could want.

Marty comes out of the kitchen, "Emmy, I need to get the rest of your stuff up here from the car so you can settle in and also get some groceries. Will you feel safe here for a while? I won't be gone long."

"I can help," I tell him, but he waves me off.

I nod and reassure him that I'll be fine and then he's off.

I love this apartment; it's just magnificent. While I wait for Marty, I invade his room. It has such a masculine vibe. His bed faces the big floor to ceiling window. Just like the living room, it's all grey with burnt orange accents. The area rug and the throw pillows on the bed are burnt orange.

When Marty arrives, I am enjoying the view from the comfy sofa. He has my meager amount of stuff on a cart much like the ones you see at a hotel. I have four suitcases and six boxes. Marty totes them up to the loft for me.

The doorbell rings while Marty is upstairs and I get up to answer it. Marty comes down the stairs at a sprint, telling me to get back from the door. Of course, I comply.

Marty talks through the door and the bellman from downstairs answers that he has the groceries that were delivered. So cool that they are delivered.

Marty brings the groceries to the kitchen and we unpack, talking about dinner. I love to cook pasta and pizzas, but Marty has bought steak and he wants to cook for me. I love a man who can cook.

Marty is so easy to be with. There are moments when he stands just a breath away that I remember the time I spent with Caesar. I even want to lean in and inhale, so I can be transported back to that sensual experience with Caesar. Marty's close resemblance to Caesar is uncanny. Marty looks kinder than Caesar, but other than that they could be twins. I wonder if that's because of how and where they were raised.

I guess I zoned out because Marty is waving his hand in front of my face saying, "Emmy are you there?"

"I'm sorry, Marty, I was daydreaming. I was thrown back to your resemblance to Caesar."

"What triggered that?" Marty asks. "Did I say or do something that brought him back in your head? Caesar is still in jail and will be there for a while."

I don't really know, so how can I tell him? I just shrug and decide to find out where things are in the kitchen so I can help cook. Marty notices my emotional confusion and doesn't push it.

My classes are easy this semester, which is great. There are so many changes in my life that something being easy is such a relief. My sorority seems to be needing me only for rush and parties, both also fairly easy. I love to plan stuff like that.

Marty has been cooking patiently while I've been daydreaming again. I look up and decide I can help with the salad prep that he has laid out. It's fun to just work at things together in content silence. Dinner is wonderful sitting at his table by the window. The amazing view as the sun sets across the city skyline makes me content. Even standing in the kitchen watching the approaching darkness makes cleanup easy.

Marty looks tired. I know he won't go to bed while I am up so I tell him I'm going to bed. He leans in and kisses me on the head and says, "Duerme bien, mi gabito."

I pull back, surprised.

Marty looks at me and apologies, "Sorry Emmy. All I said was 'sleep well, my little kitten.' I meant no harm. My mom was from Spain, so the language comes naturally to me."

My surprise and concern are written all over my face. "Really? I didn't know that. Is that why you started speaking Spanish to me when we first met? Wait, could you be related to Caesar? I mean are you related?"

His smile and wink make me smile back, but deep inside I wonder why he didn't answer me directly. I trust Marty, so I let it go.

I turn and start up the stairs to the loft, Marty steps up one stair and leans in. "Emmy, things will be ok. Don't worry too much."

Going to class with Marty in tow feels like overkill concerning security. I feel like I'm safe now that everyone is incarcerated. But it is nice to have him tag along.

My studio hours are a nice place to let myself sink into my artistic side and leave my apprehensions behind. Marty sits and reads most times I am in class.

We usually get lunch together on campus on Monday, Wednesdays, and Fridays. My classes are scheduled close together. On Tuesdays and Thursdays, I only have one class, 8:30 - 10:30 a.m., so we either eat at his place or somewhere fun.

Today, Marty wants to check out a restaurant that he's heard about, Spanish Flowers.

According to Marty, it is just good food. I like TexMex, so I am all in. The restaurant is busy but we're seated fairly quickly. Marty and I order, and comfortably begin to talk about the weekend and my commitments with the sorority and cougar mascot stuff. I keep noticing a young waiter staring at us from across the room. I have checked around to see if he can be looking at someone else, but no, it's us. It soon becomes plain that he is agitated about something.

I lean into Marty. "What's with the waiter over there?"

Marty comes very close, "Be careful, here he comes. Let me talk."

I nod and he grabs my hand like we are being intimate in conversation. He looks startled when the young boy addresses him in Spanish. Not Latin American, but Castilian, Spanish. I know a little Spanish and I think he tells Marty that he looks familiar. Marty barely looks at him and answers in just a few words. "Mucha gente dice esom". Many people say that. He then looks up and says, "Pero esta encantadora joven piensa que soy perfecta." But this lovely young woman thinks I'm perfect.

The young man actually blushes and I tilt my head in a questioning way at this display of shyness. Marty looks up again and says, "You don't speak Spanish after all?"

He quickly answers, "Si señor. Yo hablo español. Mi nombre es Manuel Moreno. Te ves como un amigo di mis hermano de España. Eres Canteras Caesar?" Yes, sir. I speak Spanish. My name is Manuel Moreno. You look like my brother's friend from Spain. Are you Caesar Canteras?

Marty looks up, winks and puts his finger to his lips. "My name here is Martin. In another life, maybe."

Manuel excuses himself and Marty leans into me so close and says, "Well, this is unnerving. Could this be a link to Caesar's friends here? We never found them you know."

Before I could answer, Manuel is back with a note that says, in English, that his brother would like Martin and the beautiful redhead to have dinner with him here tonight. "If you please." Marty smiles and answers Manuel, "I can be here, but the lady may have plans."

"My brother has heard much about your Emmy and would love to meet her." I smile and nod. Marty kicks me under the table and I try not to cry out. Manuel leaves us to make the arrangements.

We finish and head to the car where Marty lets me have it. "Emmy, what the hell did you think you were doing? I don't know how dangerous these people are and you can't be exposed like that."

Marty pulls out of the parking lot and heads to his apartment. I'm steaming. "What is so dangerous about dinner at a restaurant?"

Marty gets very quiet and doesn't answer me. In the apartment, he is on the phone immediately and fills in whoever it is on what has happened. Within thirty minutes, the doorbell is ringing and five agents arrive with suitcases in tow. I can see that a plan is in the works. I'm involved even if Marty doesn't like it.

I soon learn that there is a lot to be worried about. The location is not easy to infiltrate with agents because it's in a heavily Hispanic area so any Anglo would stick out unless dining in the restaurant. They quickly arrange a party of ten for dinner at the same time that we will be there. So Anglo agents inside and Latinos outside to watch those approaching and departing.

I will have a tracker on me in the event that we get separated. I can't imagine that I would leave Marty's side but he answers my questioning gaze with "restroom?"

"Oh, okay," I say. There is so much to go over and I'm given a paper with all of the agents photos that will be there so I will know who's a good guy and who is not.

I'm nervous and chastising myself for being so quick to answer Manuel at lunch.

I excuse myself from the team to get dressed and mentally prepare. There is a knock on the door and a female agent comes in with Marty to put the tracker in place. I think my purse but she glues it next to my belly button. So uncomfortable but necessary.

Marty waits to see if it is noticeable and does a check to see if it is easily felt through my dress. I never thought about it, but not many people check there. My dress has skinny straps and is fitted at the waist with a flared-out skirt and is deep blue. My red hair makes me easy to pick out in a crowd. Marty says they are going to portray him as Caesar's cousin. I ask him, "Why not Caesar?"

"Oh, I'm to be Caesar, but he is wanted and I'm his 'cousin', wink, wink." He uses air quotes around the word cousin. "Since you volunteered, we are going to use you as proof of who I am. I don't look so much like Caesar if you compare photos. I'll dress more like him, but you will have to help by being snuggly and dancing with me. I thought we should practice."

I turned my head, raise my eyebrow and say, "Practice snuggling?"

Marty actually blushes. The female agent, Jane, grins big. Marty recovers and says, "No, dancing. I understand Caesar can dance well. I'm a little worried. They open a dance floor at dinner time there near the bar."

"Oh, okay, let's practice. I can follow anyone."

"I am not sure I can lead."

"Really? Then I'll lead and you follow."

"Can anyone tell if I am not leading?"

"Jane, will you watch and see if you can tell? Ok, Marty, let's do this."

I step up close and Marty puts his hands on me like a fourteen-year-old boy who has never touched a girl. Jane giggles. "You're not helping, Jane. I need him to look confident and in charge." Jane giggles again. "Fat chance that's going to happen."

Jane's remark pisses off Marty enough to get him back to the take-charge guy I know. He grabs me close and takes a step as if to dance. "Wait for the music," I scold him. "We're dancing not mating."

At this, Jane burst out laughing and Marty's red hot, angry gaze sends her scampering to get out of the room. We're alone.

Wanting to get his focus back, I let some passion into my eyes and trail my hands from his hips up to his shoulders.

"I know you've wanted this from the first time I met you. Well, here I am. Willing, waiting and wanting this to go perfectly. So, enjoy this. I certainly will."

After that, dancing goes quite well. I'm pretty confident he'll pass.

Later, as we're cooling down from our dancing lessons, a thought comes to mind. "Marty, what did my parents think about this mission?"

"We sent a message, but they won't get it until this is over. Besides, you're eighteen. They technically can't stop you. That being said, I wouldn't want them angry with me so please, please be careful tonight."

"Oh, I'll be careful. We didn't necessarily go looking for this, it just happened. We're lucky that you guys had time to plan. What would have happened if his brother had been in the restaurant at lunch? No one would have had a clue how to act or plan. What a scary thought…"

TWENTY-SIX

Houston OPS

- Agent Wells and Kitten will be at Spanish Flowers tonight with a surveillance detail.
- Could have uncovered Caesar's contacts here in Houston.
- Fourteen agents will be on the ground, plus agent Wells, ten inside and four outside.

TWENTY-SEVEN

Dinner and Dancing

———

UP TO TONIGHT, THE PROSPECT of dinner and dancing would have pleased me to no end. Tonight, however, will be a new experience. I love the food at the Mexican restaurant we are heading too I worry about the company we are about to meet. This little place is in downtown Houston and is always busy. There is a small dance floor and the real Caesar loves to dance, I wonder if Marty can dance well enough to pass as Caesar who is really good at dancing. Marty and I are in his car and on our way to the restaurant. While it's nice to be on the offensive and prepared with a plan, I still feel unsettled. I think Marty's worried about me and I'm worried for him. I tell him, "If things go bad on the dance floor, I'll fake a twisted ankle and insist on sitting."

He smiles with relief and says, "Good plan."

I turn and smirk. "That's all you have? I mean, you've done this kind of stuff before. No words of wisdom?"

Marty brakes and pulls off the road to a parking lot. He almost shouts, "No. I'm worried that you, a civilian that I care about, are jumping head first into danger tonight. I know you think you're good at this, and for a civilian you are better than most. But, all kinds of shit could happen and neither of us can stop it. Please, take this seriously. It is not a game, and we will easily be outnumbered."

Marty is so angry…worried… no, terrified, that his face is purple. I turn and stare at him. I need to help him understand that I get it. I can only guess at the stress level he is under. I know I'm not experienced, but this is the one thing I can do to help catch this group here in Houston.

I lean in and take his right hand with my left hand, then use my right hand to gently pull him into a kiss. It's not a sexy kiss, but a loving one, that I hope will dial his worry back a notch. I feel him relax and pull back gently. "Emmy, I like your kisses and I understand you want me to relax and go with the flow. I'm just not sure I can. I don't work like that."

His words hit home and I realize that his worry is what keeps him alive in intense situations. I smile," I just want you to know I'm listening and will do as I'm told tonight. You are in charge and I promise to hang back and be the shy, naive girl that I'm sure Caesar described to his friends."

Marty huffs, "Well I, for one, am glad he misjudged you. You do need to play the part. Listen, but not obviously so. Be into the food and music, but listen to what is being said. It could save us both."

I turn back and look out the front window. Then it hits me, "What do I call you? Caesar? Marty? Martin? What?"

Marty starts to pull out of the parking lot and smiles, "How about mi amor? Use no names. Ok? If we are separated and there's a problem, then use Marty."

I like this plan and nod.

Marty's quiet the rest of the way. I'm wishing that Charlie and Sterling were here. The small parking lot is crowded and Marty chooses to use the valet service. No fast getaway without keys in his pocket. Marty speaks my thoughts as we pull into the restaurant parking lot. "Emmy, I know the agents with us tonight are well-trained, but I wish Charlie and Sterling were here tonight."

"Me, too," is all I can say.

The table we're seated at is set for six, not four as I expected. At least we know how many will be sitting with us, even if we don't know who. I thought Marty was going to try to resemble Caesar in dress at least, but he has come as his classy, very put together and slick self.

Manuel stops at the table, but doesn't seem to be working. He greets us and lets us know that our guests will be here shortly.

Our guests? I thought we were their guests. Oh well, go with the flow. Marty smiles at him and then back at me. Happiness all around. Yikes!

My anxiety ramps up when two couples emerge from the hostess' stand and head our way. The first, and older, couple look like they are in their late twenties, are confident and staring at us as they approach. She is a petite, Hispanic girl with large breasts and a very short dress. He is around six feet and has beautiful, black, and wavy longish hair cut close at the neck. I feel like he is trying to appeal to two different generations at once. His wavy longish hair on top like todays styles and his close cut at the ears and neck keep him with one foot in each era

The second couple looks closer to my age, I think. At least the woman looks like it. She looks like several girls I met back in Spain, with long blonde hair and lightly tanned skin. She has her hair pulled back into a severe high ponytail. Even with it pulled up, it goes well past her waist. She is a little taller than the first girl and has a well-proportioned figure. She is in all pink and looks like a delicate flower. I immediately don't trust her. The guy is also blonde and has tanned skin with athlete written all over him. His shirt is well-fitted and shows off his arm muscles. He seems less flashy than the first.

The hostess that is leading the parade looks like she could be related to the second man. Maybe brother and sister or at least cousins. Marty stands as they approach and extends his hand. "Are you Miguel?"

The older man nods and shakes hands. Manuel appears from nowhere and is making introductions. I'm worried that maybe I should recognize someone in this group, but I don't. My mind is racing as Manuel introduces Ricardo and Margarita. She smiles and says, "You know, like the drink." I smile at her, but everyone else cuts their eyes at her. I think she might not be the brightest bulb here, or she is a dang good actress.

I'm still looking for recognition of anyone that I might have met in Spain. So far, no luck. The second couple are Miguel and Mae and she says in a saccharine way with a steely undertone, "I'm not like any drink you could imagine." Yikes, scary. It's just as I thought, don't trust this one.

I hear Marty ask, "Manuel, where is your brother? This Ricardo is not your brother. I thought he was coming. I haven't seen him in nine or ten years and I bet he's changed a lot. But, not so much that I would not recognize him... I did some thinking and I think you were still picking your nose the last time I saw you. I think you would have been nine or ten."

Manuel's cheeks color as he smiles sheepishly at Marty, "You're right, I was just a little kid when I last saw you. A couple of months after I met you, I came to live with tia here in Houston. My brother will be here soon." Marty has passed the first test.

Marty continues, this time in Spanish, "Supongo que estos cuatro fueron una prueba?"

Manuel steps back a pace and lowers his head slightly, "Si."

Marty turns to me and quietly shares, "I asked Manuel whether these four were a test, to which he admits to."

When Manuel moves, I have a clear view of a man who looks to be the same age as Caesar at the hostess stand. I pat Marty's hand and point. Marty turns and smiles, "Now, that's the real Ricardo." Marty stands and waves him over.

The pretend Ricardo and Margarita move to the small table to our left which puts them in between us and our hidden-in-plain-sight agents party table. I had not looked that way yet so I was glad to see a few familiar faces. Bob is one I know well. He took me down and protected me when Caesar had me on campus the night of the kidnapping three months ago. Bob smiles big, waves, says loudly, "Hey guys, that's the cougar mascot at U of H. Hey there, Emmy. Come join our party, we're way more fun."

I freeze. I never expected anyone on the detail to speak to me. Marty looks straight at me sighs, "Go on, say hi to your fan club. I know you are well-known and it will give me a minute to reconnect with Ricardo. It's really ok." Marty and I had talked about cue words and 'really' meant it's ok and 'really, really' means get help now. I excuse myself and get up. I sort of trip over my purse as I get to my feet. I try to look nonplussed and just swing it over my shoulder and start walking. I can be so clumsy sometimes. I look back to see a couple of frowns, but I shrug and keep going.

I get to Bob and he makes a big deal about hugging me, he whispers in my ear, "Are you okay? Later, I'll appear to get drunk and come hit on you with racial slurs at the others, if needed, so I can be close enough to take you away. Don't worry, that won't happen unless things get messy."

I smile and nod as he releases me. Bob begins with introductions to everyone at the table. He ends his conversation with, "Emmy is my next girlfriend when she gets tired of that bozo."

Wow, those are fighting words. Every head from my table turns to frown at him then swivel to Marty. Marty gets up and walks over and says, "Sadly for you, she is very happy with this bozo, so back off." Ricardo and fake Ricardo are at his shoulder. I step around Bob and put both hands on Marty and push him back a small step.

"Come on, my silly Bozo, Come clown around with me." Thank God, everyone laughs and we go back to the table arm in arm.

What was that all about? I'm sure there's a reason but I definitely don't get it. Marty leans in as he pushes my chair in and says, "Bob put a small gun in your handbag. He says you told him you know how to use it?"

I smile a sensual smile and plant a kiss on him and say, "Yes, mi amor. I know how to use you." All the men laugh, Margarita smiles, but Mae has a cold look on her face. The real Ricardo has a stunning young woman on his arm that seems to be in her own private world and not interested in any of us. She is introduced as Cecilia and holds on tight to Ricardo. He treats her like a precious gem. I'm impressed. He might have a heart, at least for her.

We all sit and enjoy a pleasant meal. I'm not too hungry, but I do my best to eat and remember to call Marty, mi amor. It would be easier to enjoy this and relax if I didn't have a viper sitting across from me named Mae. She has smiled to others, but for me she has the look of a snake ready to strike.

Finally, Mae speaks. She tells me she knows I can dance. "You don't remember me, do you?"

Holy shit, should I know her? It's been two and a half years since I was in Spain and right now, that seems like a lifetime ago.

I must look surprised because she continues, "I was the little girl you dismissed in 'The White Horse', the club in Salamanca." She points at Marty as she continues to speak. "I was sixteen, just like you, and you so disgracefully flirted with both Caesar and Carlos."

She has clearly accepted Marty as Caesar because she indicated that "we" danced by pointing at him when referencing Caesar. Marty puts his hand on my hand and holds it. I take a deep breath and extend an honest statement to her, hoping she will simmer down.

"Mae, I do remember you. Truthfully, I thought you were much younger than sixteen. I'm sorry you felt that I was after both. Truth be told, Carlos always felt like a brother to me. Caesar, he was that exciting, bad boy that tempted me. I'm so surprised that you and I get to meet once again and excited to get to know you, woman to woman." I smile as nice and sincere as I can. I can see her soften slightly.

Marty steps into the conversation with, "I would have never recognized you. How could I have missed such a beauty as you?"

Her head immediately swivels his way and through gritted teeth, she says, "You, don't talk to me. You are not trustworthy with women of any age. I am concerned for Emmy, that she is connected with you in any way. Carlos told me she is from a good and famous family. You are a street mongrel."

At this Ricardo stands and takes her by the hand, leading to the dance floor. There is a lovely, slow dance playing and Marty stands and leads me to the floor, too. I am nervous for us. He pulls me into his arms and we dance.

Marty has lied to me, he can dance. I lean in and whisper, "You can dance, mi amor." He kisses me on the forehead and smiles. I have secrets, too. I want to put his dancing skills to the test, but not tonight.

After the dance, Mae grabs my hand and leads me to the women's restroom. I want to resist as I'm kind of frightened of her. For all her beauty, she seems deadly.

Once inside, she checks the place over for people and bugs, I guess. I decide to help. She rolls her eyes at me and I say, "What? Can't I help you?"

Mae backs me against the wall and says, "Why are you here? I mean, are you crazy? Who is that man with you? I know he is not Caesar but a close duplicate."

To say I am stunned is an understatement. I start to talk but all that comes out is confused, jumbled syllables.

"Just as I thought, you are winging this," she huffs. "You are in over your head. Go home little girl, leave this to the professionals." Mae backs up a pace and puts her hands on her hips this time waiting for an answer.

Professionals, what professionals? There is a table full of them out there and she is not one of them, or is she? I stammer and then ask. "Who do you work for? What is going on here? I don't know what you mean."

Mae takes a deep breath, "I am a good guy in this situation and who I work for is none of your business. When you leave tonight, don't come back here. I have protected you by not reveling your fake but after tonight you are on your own and, for that matter, so is he."

All of a sudden, she leans in and says, "Are you wired?"

She pushes me against the wall and starts to touch me everywhere. Her hand lands on my belly area and gasps.

"Who is listening? You are even more than stupid coming to this group with a wire. Be glad I brought you to the restroom instead of one of the others. Cecilia would have turned you over to the men, but Margarita would have gutted you right here and now without a thought. She is crazy."

I take a breath to answer, when the door opens and in walks two of the girls from Bob's table. They look at us, frown, and begin applying lipstick and fixing their hair.

I look straight into the mirror and say to Mae, "I understand what you want and I will talk to mi amor on the way home. I am listening to you."

I can see the two girls in my peripheral vision relax. One whispers to the other, then they both giggle and leave.

I am not sure if Marty has convinced them he is Caesar, but

all feels okay when I get back to the table.

As we get up to leave, Bob approaches and declares in a seriously drunk voice, "I need to get a good night kiss from my Emmy." His friends try to restrain him, but he breaks loose. As he comes closer, Ricardo steps in his way. Bob loses balance and falls into Ricardo only to be delivered back to his friends. All of Ricardo's friends laugh and Bob's friends take him away. What was that about?

I can't wait to get away from them and talk to Marty. We are back in the car and I want to talk. Marty puts his finger to my mouth and shows me a small thing in his pocket. He leans in and plants a kiss on me and says, "I have made special plans for us tonight. I want to be alone with you."

By this time, he has written what I should say on a post-it note. I read it aloud. "I'm all yours, mi amor." We drive a few miles to the museum district of Houston and pull into the Warwick Hotel across the fountain from the museum and Rice University. The hotel is expecting us because at the mention of Caesar Cantera, Marty is handed keys and we are escorted to a private keyed elevator.

I am quiet the whole way to the room, which is unsurprisingly full of silent people as we enter. I need a drink…I mean, I really need a drink. I sit and wait for someone to start talking.

Marty holds up his hand, all remain silent. "Ricardo, hasta aquí entras en mi vida privada. Emmy y yo estaremos un poco preocupados por el resto de la noche."

He turns to me and says "Emmy, I said this is as far as Ricardo can enter into my private life, and that we'll be a little preoccupied for the rest of the night." With a wink, Marty drops the device he had shown me earlier into a glass of water.

TWENTY-EIGHT

Houston OPS

- Warwick Hotel suite is set up for tonight's debriefing.
- Kitten and agent Wells will stay the night together as cover.
- The security team from the restaurant will come to this meeting. Bob attached a tracker to Ricardo when he fell into him. Outside agents will track him.
- Outside surveillance teams will stay with their assigned suspects and report as needed.
- Intel on Marcelo Ramirez, Margarita Molina, Cecelia Quintero, Ricardo, and Manuel Moreno is needed as soon as possible.
- Intel on Mae is scarce for now. Her Italian passport is Mary Madelyn Vicinti. She is distantly related to Serge and Beate Klarsfeld of France. They brought Klaus Barbie, the butcher of Lyon to trial. They are well known for hunting Nazis.
- As per her conversation with Kitten at the restaurant, she is working some angle in this mess.
- Her surveillance team is to bring her in if possible

TWENTY-NINE

The Warwick

THE GROUP HERE IN THE suite is working at full speed. I'm exhausted, but I know I can't just flake out, even though I sure want to. Bob shows up with his team and I am rewarded with a big hug from him and high fives from the two girls from the restroom. Bob starts with, "I think we should sign Emmy up to work with us."

Marty's head whips around. "You have not met her mother. She would not approve. Just for the record, I would not want to cross her, she can be scary."

The two girls, Susan and Julie, defend Bob's assessment of my skills. Susan speaks first, "Emmy, you handled the restroom encounter as if you were a professional. We were ready to start a girl fight right then and there, but you defused the situation with the correct words to make us stand down. Bravo."

"I think she was amazing when she endured Bob's groping hello hug," added Julie.

I snicker at this. "The last time I had an encounter with Bob, he pulled me to the ground and landed on top of me, so this didn't seem all that bad in comparison."

Bob smiles. "See, she likes me!"

That small conversation seemed to break the tension. I sit down in the sitting area of the suite and just listen. Every once in a while, I'm asked my opinion. I didn't need to recap the restroom conversation because of the tracker/receiver attached to my belly. All the talk about the receiver inspires me to go to the bathroom and attempt to remove it. I guess I'm gone too long because Susan knocks on the door and asks, "you okay, Emmy?"

I jump at her knock, which causes me to rip the device off. It hurts like a sticky band-aid coming off. I yelp loudly and she flies in, looking ready for anything. When she sees what I'm doing, she smiles and says, "for future reference, there is an easier way to do that. I have some lotion that will help with that patch of damaged skin."

I thank her for the offer and look down to inspect the damage. There's no blood, but some very irritated skin.

Susan continues, "Things have calmed down out there and moved to the other side of the suite so you might actually get some rest now. Marty is staying if you want him to, and the rest of the team is either staying in the other suite or is rotating out with the surveillance teams."

I don't know how I feel about all of this, but it is nice to have another woman to talk to. I start with, "Susan, will you be close or are you on one of the rotating teams for surveillance?"

She smiles and says, "I have the sofa on this side of the suite so if you want to talk just come get me. I've read your file and I admire your courage. I'm not so sure I could continue with this craziness like you are."

I thank her and say that I plan to take her up on that talk soon but for now, I need to close my eyes. She leaves, but stops in the doorway. "Marty wants to talk. Should I tell him tomorrow or now?"

I smile and look past her. "We're a team, so now is good." I can see Marty smile and start walking my way. Susan excuses herself to the other room and Marty lets her pass and closes the door behind him.

I look at Marty and sigh, "What next? I think I need some sleep but I'm not sure I will without knowledge of what's to come."

Marty moves to the window and opens the drapes to reveal the lights from the Medical Center. I don't care what city you are in, there is always a surreal view from so high up at night. This night seems to have more mystery out there. I walk over and stand next to him and say, "Tell me what happened when I was in the restroom with Mae."

Marty chuckled to himself. "I thought that all the girls were going to the restroom at once when you and Mae disappeared inside. Margarita and Cecilia started to get up but Ricardo quashed that saying Mae could handle you."

The two from Bob's table did go in and were out pretty quick and unruffled. I knew someone at Bob's table was monitoring your bug so I knew if things went sideways, or if you were in trouble, they would react.

I turn and face Marty, "I meant what happened at your table with you while I was gone."

He smirks again. "Well, as you know, Mae not calling me out as a fake made it easy for me to find out what they needed or wanted. I am accepted as authentic and have made plans to catch up with them sometime tomorrow."

I am looking straight out the window but in my reflection, he can see me cut my eyes his way. He winks and says, "You are not invited. Not my choice, even though I am glad, but because it is business and the girls aren't invited. Mae's insight into the other two girls was helpful and she is right in her appraisal of them. Both are dangerous in different ways."

"Do you mind if I keep the drapes open tonight?" I ask. I turn and walk back to the bed intending to lay down. Marty watches me the whole way. When I look back, he is still staring.

"What?"

Marty sputters and then, "You want me to stay in here with you? I mean, I can. I thought you might need a break from all this doom and gloom stuff, me included."

I sit up, almost panicking at the thought of not having him in the room, when I realize I have never told him how safe he makes me feel. Since that first day I met him and he startled me with his resemblance to Caesar, I have never reassured him that I now can tell the difference anywhere.

I'm not sure how he'll take my explanation, but I jump right in. "Marty, I've grown to depend on you. I trust you and right now would feel lost if you weren't with me. I don't care where you sleep, as long as it's in this room. This king-size bed is big enough for both of us to sleep and not even bump into each other. If you would rather sleep on the sofa over there, then so be it. I promise not to take advantage of you if you choose the bed."

Marty roars with laughter. As he recovers from his laughing fit, he explains, "I think I can handle any advances you aim at me and I would rather sleep next to you so I can feel you if you make any sudden moves. A good night sleep is what I need and Susan is just outside the door for protection."

I cock my head. "You need protection?"

Marty winks. "Maybe."

THIRTY

Houston OPS

- We have three residences to check out. I need all the paperwork you can put together on who comes and goes.
- Still waiting on Mary Madelyn Vicinti, AKA Mae, intel from Interpol.
- Kitten is at the Warwick with Susan until Marty returns.
- Big Bird and Whitey understand our needs last night and are on board.
- Reports on each of last night's players: Margarita Molina and Marcelo Ramirez are both from the Laredo area and have extensive juvenile records. Miguel Martin is from the Houston area and is muscle for Ricardo. Ricardo Moreno and his brother Manuel grew up here in Texas but the rest of their family live in Guadalajara, Mexico, and both visit there often. Locals are building a case on this whole group's heavy involvement in drug trafficking.

THIRTY-ONE

Valentine's

CHARLIE IS BACK AND BOY am I glad. Sterling looks like he was in a bar fight and I soon find out he was. Sterling heads for the kitchen where Marty is making lunch. Charlie and I are snuggling on the sofa. I just want to sit, talk and be close. We talk about Jim, and that awkward dinner at the restaurant. As far as I can tell, Jim will probably get an up-close and personal meeting with Charlie, Marty, and Sterling at some point. As far as the development with Ricardo, Mae, and that whole crowd... that is another thing altogether.

Marty and Mae have met at headquarters and seem to have made peace, considering Marty is not Caesar at all. In public, Mae maintains the ruse that he is Caesar and to that end, she continues to be hostile with him.

On the other hand, Mae has been pleasant with me and seems to have explained to the others that I'm okay, if not a little naive or lovestruck with Caesar. Margarita thinks that Caesars looks make him good enough to keep, if for nothing else than the eye candy and, of course, sex. She is so vulgar that she makes me blush. Cecilia is at least pleasant and talks about fashion and restaurants. I haven't figured her out yet. I have only been out with the girls once since the initial meeting and it was very nerve-racking.

Valentine's Day is in two days and I need to shop for some goodies for my boys. I have my head on Charlie's shoulder thinking of what to buy Marty and Sterling. I expect that Charlie and I will go out to dinner or at least have a cozy dinner in…alone. I turn to Charlie and ask, "What do you want to do for Valentine's day? Some of my sorority sisters and dates are going out together, but that's not very romantic. I want alone time with you."

Charlie stiffens as Marty comes around the corner with muffins for everyone.

"Didn't Charlie inform you that on that special night, I have a date with you? Your presence and Marty, AKA mi amor AKA Caesar, are expected to be out with our new friends."

I turn to Charlie for confirmation. "Wait, what?! I want to be with you… all night."

He smiles and says, "Marty needs his Emmy that evening for show. I will be watching, but close."

This is not what I want. Charlie doesn't seem too happy either.

Charlie tries to change the subject. "Susan wants to go shopping with you and your sisters for a new dress for the date. I'm not invited. She would like to go today."

He can tell I am disappointed and want him. He also knows me well enough that I will comply and do my best.

"As far as Valentine's evening, I promise I will be close. And if you think I'd let Marty be alone with you for too long, you're nuts. When you buy this dress, I'll know it's for me, and not anyone else."

He's rambling on and on, so I put my finger across his lips, then replace my finger with my lips as I press into him. Of course, that's when Marty chooses to walk over closer and say, "Is this what you meant you would do when you said you'd take advantage of me? Man, I should have let you."

Charlie looks from me to Marty and then back with a raised eyebrow.

I sigh. "Charlie, he's messing with your head. Ignore him and put your lips back where they were. Just pretend he's not here. Maybe he'll learn something from watching."

At this, Charlie laughs and Sterling steps in from behind Marty and chimes in, "ouch, our little Emmy has truly grown up."

"So, when do I leave to shop? Didn't Susan's cover get compromised when she was at the Mexican restaurant?" I ask this because I like Susan and wouldn't want her in the crosshairs of this group. Charlie answers, "She might be recognized, but her presence can be explained away because you did get introduced that night. And besides, it is her job. She won't be going with you. You'll 'bump' into her while shopping and invite her to join you."

"Okay, I can see that, but is it enough for these nervous guys and weirder girlfriends you are trying to smoke out? Mae still scares me and up until I had read the intel on the Klarsfelds of France, I wasn't just scared, but terrified, of that vibe of hers. I'm so glad you gave me the intel to read. I learned a lot about her relative, Serge Klarsfeld, like how he's a Romanian-born French activist and a Nazi hunter like Mom and Dad."

"He is known for documenting the Holocaust to establish a written record," said Sterling. "Those archives will assist in the prosecution of war criminals. Oh, and he and his wife have been at this for a while, since the early sixties I think. Their records are, for now, the best source we have of the Jewish victims of German-occupied France."

"And they are active supporters of Israel," I add.

"Well, look at you. I thought I was the expert," Sterling continues. "Did you read his family history, too?"

I smile and continue, "Why yes, I did."

I nearly stood up, like I was in class doing a history presentation, but caught myself and just snuggled in a little closer to Charlie as I recited what I'd learned.

"Ok, so Serge Klarsfeld was born in Bucharest, Romania, into a family of Romanian Jews. They moved to France before the Second World War began. In mid-1943, his father was arrested by the SS in Nice, France during a roundup ordered by Brunner. His dad was deported to the Auschwitz concentration camp where he died. Young Serge landed in a home for Jewish children operated by the OSE, this group that rescued children from the Nazis. Let's see… His mom and sister also survived the war in Vichy, France. They were helped by the underground French Resistance that began in late 1943."

"Pretty good, for a junior agent," Sterling says.

"I don't think you should encourage Emmy that way," Marty,

ever the cautious one, says. "Her mom and dad are not all that happy she is involved again."

Sterling steps up close to Marty and shakes his head at him. "I know you think discouraging Emmy will keep her out of this, but as you can see it isn't working. Besides, knowledge is power. The more she knows the safer she is."

Time for me to step in. "Boys, I get it. This could be dangerous and I'm already involved, so I need to know as much as possible. I don't want to get caught in over my head just because I didn't know."

Charlie has been quiet this whole time, so when he speaks I'm startled. "Emmy, I think you should know as much as possible, too, but if you seem to know too much then one of them may think you are involved in this more than an innocent bystander. That idea scares me."

I look straight into Charlie's eyes as I respond. "I'm sure you're right, Charlie. I'll be sure to keep my mouth shut and play dumb when I'm not with you guys."

Charlie is quiet but Marty says, "This what we do know. Marcelo is protection and is good at it. He's not too bright, but definitely excels at the physical stuff. Margarita has a juvenile record from high school. She's known for instigating fights and winning. They're an item and have been for a while. Mae is in it for the intel. Miguel is second-in-command and deadly, but Mae seems to be his Achilles' heel. He's been arrested several times but has been released because of insufficient evidence. He seems to be Ricardo's bodyguard of sorts. Cecilia is a Mexican national here on a student visa. She is from a prominent family in Guadalajara and is meant to be Ricardo's arranged wife. Ricardo is the boss, at least of the younger crowd. I believe there is another older group of men who have the final say on important matters."

My head is swimming. I lean back and lay my head on the sofa and close my eyes. I feel Charlie lean in close. I guess he's worried again. I open my eyes and he is indeed right there. "Look, I'm glad you have gotten this group figured out this far, but what more do you need? I get that Marty, as Caesar, could get you all the intel you need about the Ratline here in the U.S., but how is that going to work? I mean, doesn't everyone on the Spanish side of this really know that Max, Carlos, Caesar, and company are guests of the United States government? How can Marty's cover be maintained and to what end?"

Marty answers, "Yes and no. The connection to the cartel in Mexico is another piece to the puzzle that has not been connected until now. The authorities here in Texas and the Feds want to know more. Infiltrating them is difficult and, dare I say, deadly. The opportunity to get this close cannot be ignored. Mae is in and is willing to help. That help doesn't come along too often."

I am nodding my head. I get that this is important. I put a finger in the air. "I'm sure Mae has many reasons for her passion with this, maybe even a self-made mission, but all this info still doesn't make me dial back my fears about her. I know my life is different than most teens, but it's not tainted by hatred. Sad that hers appears to be. I know now why I'm needed. I am here to help open the door again." I lean into Charlie and he does the same.

Charlie speaks into my hair, "You're right not to trust Mae. She is very connected to the Klarsfelds and they are still very active in France. I mean, just recently Klarsfeld was considering kidnapping Barbie, just like the Mossad did with Eichmann. So far, his plan has been unsuccessful. For now, his group has decided to just bring international pressure trying to force his extradition."

Sterling comes over to the loveseat next to the window, sofa, and glass wall. He plops down and says, "Mae appears to be a relative and embedded in that organization's beliefs and goals. She is here in Houston going to college. We think this is when she ran into this subgroup of the Ratlines. I am sure with her strong beliefs she couldn't help but infiltrate this group."

"I know Ratlines are a system of escape routes for Nazis and other fascists fleeing Europe during the aftermath of World War II. Mom and Dad have used this intel to help in their assignments. These escape routes mainly lead toward havens in Latin America, particularly Argentina, Chile, Paraguay, Colombia, Brazil, Uruguay, Mexico, Peru, Guatemala, Ecuador, and Bolivia, as well as the United States, Spain, and Switzerland.

Wow, that feels like half the world."

Marty adds, "Yes, you're right, Emmy. There are two primary routes: the first from Germany to Spain, then Argentina; the second from Germany to Rome to Genoa, then South America. The two routes developed independently but eventually came together. Your parents are at the Argentina end to watch and report. So, if something slows them down, or distracts them then bad people could slip through. You being in danger distracts them from this mission."

I sigh, "Okay, I get that now, but is there a 'Ratline' connection here in Texas or at least the U.S.?"

Sterling looks at me, "We have known for a long time that there is a great possibility of groups here in the U.S., but until you two stumbled into this one we thought they were small, unused and unorganized. This group looks to have more than one focus. The Ratline is more of a job than a passion. Their other focus is on drugs from Mexico. Caesar's presence is like Ratline royalty appearing at the door. They were as unprepared for him as you were when you were recognized in the restaurant. According to Mae, it spooked them."

I am hoping I can remember all this. It is good for me that the boys are going over what I read, maybe it will sink in.

"I don't know how the Ratline got here, or why, but there is a connection. We have stumbled into it and need to be careful. This group is not playing games," explains Marty.

I look at all three and raise my hand. They stop and look my way. I feel foolish all of a sudden.

"Ah, so, is this where Caesar's family, the Italian Ratline and Carlos's family, the Spanish Ratline connected years ago?"

Charlie answers this time, "Well, not here in Texas, but they connected probably in Argentina. We know the Ratlines were supported by clergy of the Catholic Church, and even supported by the Vatican. It makes sense when you consider both Spain and Italy have strong Catholic ties and so does South America."

I am a little confused so I ask, "Okay, so what's with the part about Hitler and the Ratlines?"

"I got this," Sterling says. "While the Nazi leader, Adolf Hitler, is considered by reputable informants to have committed suicide in Berlin near the end of the war, various conspiracy theories claim that he survived the war and fled to Argentina through the Ratlines."

No wonder my parents are in South America a lot. I am quiet for a minute, but when I look up all eyes are on me. I smile. "That makes sense. So, Mae befriended Ricardo to get intel back to France and now we have crossed paths with them, too?" This is so complicated and feels like a never-ending circle.

Sterling has moved and is sitting next to me, quite close. I cut my eyes at him. "Why are you so close?" He smiles and comes in closer.

"You told Charlie to ignore us, that we might learn something. I'm the kind of learner that does better up close and hands-on." Charlie reaches over and shoves him off the edge of the sofa.

I think I could spend all day listening and still not learn it all. I can see why the boys are worried I will stick my foot in my mouth. The stress of this shopping spree is becoming very real to me. All I can do is pray and focus on the task at hand. I love to shop, but not so much today.

THIRTY-TWO

Houston OPS

- Kitten is out with the group, shopping. Sterling, Charlie and Susan are on this assignment.
- Susan and Sterling are both going to attempt to fit into the group during shopping.
- Marty is hanging out with Ricardo and the others for the afternoon.
- Kitten has commitments to the basketball game tonight. The game is in town. Campus security has been alerted.
- Intel on anyone who approaches the group. We need to keep an updated list of all players and get this group documented. We'll be handing off this investigation to local authority.
- In the interim, we will continue to secure our assets. Agent Martin Wells will be on special assignment with the local FBI until further notice. He will report intel to both teams.

THIRTY-THREE

Shopping and the Game

MARTY BROUGHT OUT HIS CAR for this. I think it's his, but maybe not. Note to self, ask. He is taking me to the entrance of the mall where I'm to meet the girls. He won't be staying with me, but there will be a security detail. Theirs, not ours. Somewhere nearby, there will be our people, blending in. Marty is meeting up with Ricardo.

Sterling and Susan will attempt to join our trip today. Charlie wanted the job of being inserted, but our attachment to each other might compromise this. I'm glad he'll be watching from afar and not up close. I don't want to blow this because I've missed him so much and I unconsciously reach out to touch him.

As we pull up to the Galleria's entrance on the Westheimer side, I can feel my heartbeat quicken. As I'm looking around for anyone I might recognize, Marty unexpectedly reaches over and pulls me close for a kiss, which I instinctively resist.

We are lip to lip when he nuzzles my cheek and says, "Make this believable, we are being watched." I hadn't seen anyone, but I guess he had. I lean in and while it's not passionate, it should certainly be believable. Just as we release the kiss, my door is opened and I jump. It's fake Ricardo and Mae, Margarita, and Cecilia. They are all smiling at my surprise, except Mae of course.

Margarita winks and says, "Don't let us stop you. I like watching."

Ick, she likes to watch. What other kinds of weird things does she like? Who knows? Shopping today will be interesting. Four females all with different tastes and styles should be amusing.

I step out of the car, and per Houston's unpredictable weather in February, it begins to rain. All of us hurry to take cover. As I turn, I meet Marty's worried eyes as he waves. In my heart, I'm terrified. As we step inside, I wonder how and when I will bump into Susan. She is a beautiful lean girl, about twenty-three, I think. She went straight out of college into the service and is from Virginia, currently assigned here. She speaks three languages, Spanish and Italian, and of course English, with a barely noticeable Southern drawl. I'm jealous, I need to practice my Spanish.

Cecilia and Mae are ahead of me and I'm left with the not-so-bright Margarita and her fake Ricardo. Ricardo, I guess, is our protection. He is tall and muscular, and Margarita is hanging on him. She is either in love or lust, I can't tell which. When fake Ricardo speaks, I smile at him and this politeness must be interpreted as flirting because she stops and steps in close.

"This man is mine. Don't get any ideas about him. I can make you uncomfortable without killing you." I can't believe she mentioned killing. I am not interested in this mafia looking goon. I do my best to be contrite and start with, "Margarita, I'm not interested in your man. I have quite a man myself. Mi amor is all I need."

With this is straightforward declaration, she steps back and says calmly, "Let's catch up with the others. Oh and by the way, his real name is Marcelo, not Ricardo. That was just for the test at the restaurant." I should have guessed that was not his name. Ok, that makes it easier. I'm more than happy to catch up with the others.

Our first stop is Mae's favorite place to shop and we sort of spread out to look through the racks. I had been briefed with gestures to signal Charlie or anyone else watching if I needed help. I told them to just stick with a few signals, as I would hate to accidentally use one and not mean it. So, we decided on three. I am glad they are things that are not natural gestures for me. It worries me I would falsely signal. One was 'help, and I need help now.' To signal this, I was to just sit down on something unusual even if it was all the way to the floor. Second, 'I'm worried, so come in closer.' For this one, I am to feign a coughing fit. And third, 'I'm okay.' For this, I drop my purse on the floor, retrieve it and say, "I'm ok." All seemed easy enough. I wonder what Charlie's thoughts would be about Margarita's jealous fit and declaration of killing me.

There are lots of dresses here, but none that are for me. Margarita finds a sexy, skimpy dress that would count as foreplay. This dress is a tiny scrap of black Lycra, like bathing suit material, with red roses embroidered around the top and bottom. To say that it is form-fitting is an understatement. Ricardo, I mean Marcelo, is very interested in when and where she is planning on wearing it. This is when I really realize he is mostly muscle with not too much brainpower. Come on, man. We're shopping for Valentine's Day dresses for the party tomorrow.

Mae puts two dresses on hold, but Cecilia is not finding a thing and neither am I. On to the next place. Cecilia wants to go to Neiman Marcus, but I think Lord and Taylor is the store for me. They are at opposite ends of the mall, so we have our work cut out for us. Neiman Marcus has just what Cecilia wants, so she's more than happy to shop for jewelry and shoes now. I already have shoes, jewelry and a dress, but Marty tells me to buy something anyway. I questioned him about why I needed to buy a dress and he just said to just buy the sexiest, best thing I saw that felt good to dance in. So, off to Lord and Taylor with many stops along the way for other things.

Mae has bought a Coach purse and we are stepping back into the mall when I hear my name. Susan is approaching me, and Marcelo steps in close. I wave him back and say, "Don't make a scene, she's harmless. Remember, she's from the other night at the restaurant? You know, with the drunk guy's group?"

I feel him relax a little, but he turns to me and says, "Well, what does she want?"

I step back and look as innocent as I can. "She's a new friend, so she's probably just being friendly. Not everyone is a threat."

"Hi, Susan. What brings you here?"

She smiles and says, "Just shopping. Dad sent some money for me to buy myself something cute for Valentine's Day. I didn't have the heart to tell him I have nowhere to go, but I'm going to buy a dress anyways. I'll call him and tell him about it, and send him a photo. With mom gone, I'm all he has to spoil and so I let him. What are you up to?"

"I am shopping for a dress, too. We're heading to Lord and Taylor. You're welcome to tag along if you want. Oh, how rude. Do you remember my friends from the restaurant?"

Everyone is staring at her. She smiles and looks past me, "I remember their faces but we were never introduced. Hi everyone, I'm Susan Johnson."

Before anyone has a chance to object, I begin introductions, "Susan, this is Mae Vicinti, she goes to U of H, too, and is from Spain, or is it France? I can't remember."

Mae nods, "I'm from France, but lived in Spain for a while in Malaga."

Oh, okay news to me. I continue, "This is Cecilia Quintero and she lives here, I think."

Cecilia nods, "I'm here for now. My family wants me to come home to Guadalajara, but I like it here."

I press on in my introductions. "And then this is Margarita Molina and Marcelo Rameriez, both from Texas near Laredo. They are an item, so no flirting." I finish with a wink.

Susan turns to Margarita and says, "I am not into stealing boyfriends, no matter how cute they are, so no worries from me. I'm just impressed that he's willing to shop with y'all. Did I say that 'y'all' right? I am from Northern Virginia and while it is considered the South, not all say that."

I turn to walk and talk, and so does Susan. I don't plan to let anyone stopping her from joining us and no one does. I can see Mae looking her up and down but Susan doesn't even let on she notices.

After a few more stops, we make it to Lord and Taylor's dress section. Cecilia pulls out a dress and says. "Emmy, this looks like you. I think you should try it on." Impressed that Cecilia has spoken to me directly, I answer, " Thanks! I think you might be right, this is my style. How did you know?"

I'm surprised again when she informs me that she is studying fashion and art in college and has seen my work in lab time.

I step back, I am sure my mouth is open and a million things run through my mind. Is she in my lab class and I have never noticed? Classes now or last semester, when the boys were with me? I try to look as natural as I can, even though my brain is terrified, as I ask, "Which lab are we in together?"

"I have been the model in your life drawing class this semester. It is how I make money. Thank you for not mentioning it around the others." Wow, she sure has been! I study and sketch the models, but I'm usually focused on the structure and drawing, not at the actual living person in front of me. I blush, feeling guilty I hadn't made the connection.

Cecilia smiles and says, "I realized just recently that the art students in those classes are not even aware that I am a person. Most, like you, are focused on what they are putting on paper, not me. I was terrified, at first, being naked but soon learned no one even remembers me. So, no worries. Here is another dress you might like."

I smile and move towards the dressing room. Cecilia continues picking out things to try on and chooses some for Mae and Margarita. They are comfortable with each other. They clearly shop together often.

With both of her choices and several others, I enter the dressing room with Susan in tow. Susan has a few to try on, too. Cecilia's choices are nice, but one just doesn't do anything for me. The three black dresses I have chosen are so much like ones I have. I try on the first dress Cecilia gave me, thinking I won't be finding something to buy. This dress looks so old school, like something my mom might wear. I can hear the others in the dressing room as they step out to show off what they have on.

Susan has stepped into the area with the big mirror with the other girls and they are chatting about the party. Margarita is enjoying Susan's attention. I think most of the others look down at Margarita so she seems to be enjoying Susan's attention. I can hear Margarita tell Susan her dress is perfect. Susan answers, "Yes, is it lovely, but this Valentine's it will be staying in the closet, I have nowhere to go, and no one to go with." I know she's fishing for an invite to the party tomorrow and she gets it. I'm about to open the door when I hear Mae say, "Don't come with a date. There will be plenty of unattached men there, and cute ones, to boot." They all giggle.

I can't get the zipper up on this dress, so I open the door, step out and ask, "Can someone zip this up for me?"

I'm holding on to the dress in front because it has the tiniest rhinestone straps. As I turn to look, I see the surprise on everyone's face. It feels custom-made for me, and when I look in the big mirrors it's as though I'm looking at a younger version of my mom. Yikes, did I just think that? I hope I didn't say that out loud. As much as I love my mom, I do not want to look like her.

This is the dress that Cecilia handed me first and it fits like a glove. It is a pink and rose large-flowered print. It has a waist and then it is slightly gathered around the waist with a light net underneath to give it body. The hem is not straight across at the bottom which hits about an inch above my knees. It is like the bottom of Cinderella's blue dress in the animated version of Disney's film. I guess you call it scalloped. I love it. I will have to find shoes for it now.

Margarita is the first to speak, "I will have to tie Marcelo to me to keep him in control." Everyone laughs. Cecilia is smiling. "I guess my choice is a winner."

Mae is smiling, too. "Cecilia picked mine out, too. She is good at this." I agree, she has talent.

I turn to Susan, "I hear you're invited to the party, too?" She nods. "Are you going to drive or can we come get you?" Susan smiles, "I would love to ride with you if you think your guy wouldn't mind."

I nod, and say "No problem at all, but I need to look at some shoes for this dress. It deserves the right ones. Cecilia, can you help?" She smiles and plans are made to meet in the shoe department as soon as we are all dressed.

Marcelo is sitting in the shoe department with all the packages. He makes a good packhorse. Margarita rewards his efforts with a kiss and a pat on his cute butt. She catches me watching and I lean in and explain, "Just window shopping, I plan on buying at home."

I guess she has never heard that expression before because she explodes with laughter. I shake my head and walk towards other displays of delicate heels. I need the perfect shoes.

The other girls are curious about what is so funny. Margarita begins to tell them when I spot one of the cheerleaders from the squad. He has a broken arm. That's new. I wave at him and he approaches. Again, Marcelo stands. I explain we are on the same cheerleading squad and he is harmless. Mike comes over and we both look down at his arm. "How? I mean when? Are you okay?"

He smiles and winks, "I was roughhousing at the frat house and fell. This is the result. I'll be out for the rest of the basketball season. I have six weeks in the cast and then they say I won't be strong enough to lift anyone in a stunt for another month. School will be out for the semester before I'll be released. But no worries, there's a sub from the gymnastic team who's going to finish the season in my place. I am sure you'll meet him tonight."

What was the wink about? I know Mike has a fiancée, so what gives?

All the girls have circled us and are offering to sign his cast. He loves the attention. He indulges their requests to sign his cast, but I can tell he wants phone numbers. Not for himself but for his frat brothers. Boy, is he going to be disappointed when I explain that all of them are taken. I'm not going to burst that bubble yet. Just let him enjoy the attention. Susan is beaming. I'm missing something here. Mike excuses himself and waves with his casted arm as he goes up the escalator.

Cecilia is good at finding just the right things for everyone, including the perfect shoes for me. I like this girl. There is, however, something amiss with her. I just can't put my finger on it. Marcelo announces he's hungry and thinks the new restaurant, Farrell's Ice Cream Parlor, will be perfect. I need actual lunch, not just ice cream, but he explains that they serve good hamburgers in addition to ice cream. Everyone else thinks this is a great idea, so who am I to turn down ice cream?

He's right. Farrell's has good food and we watch as ice cream dishes called the "Pig's Trough" and "The Zoo," both giant-sized ice cream delights, are delivered to tables. Of course, Marcelo gets the "Pig's Trough" and Margarita helps him devour it. I'm full just thinking about it.

At one point, I find myself reliving the whipped cream experience with Jim. I must have a disturbed look because Susan asks me if I'm alright. I nod, but she pointedly looks at the ice cream dish in front of Marcelo and Margarita and just says, "I understand."

She understands? What does she understand? I sure hope that experience with Jim is not in some report for just anyone to read. If it is, I will personally kill Marty for that intrusion.

She asks again if I'm sure, but before I can answer, Marcelo tunes in, looks alert and asks, "Is there something wrong? Am I missing something?"

He has ice cream on the edge of his mouth and Margarita uses her napkin to fix that. I giggle and respond, "Marcelo, nothing is wrong. I was just daydreaming. It's a bad habit, but stand down."

I notice the time and say, "Guys, I have to get home, then to the gym to get ready for the game tonight."

Susan responds first, "Where's home? Did you drive here? I have my car, so I can take you if you didn't."

"Hold your horses. Let me make a call and see what everyone else has in mind." With that comment, Marcelo hops up and heads for the hostess stand. I see her offer the phone to him. He dials and appears to be deep in conversation.

"Susan, I live between here and Rice University. The Coogs are playing a team from Louisiana tonight, Loyola I think. Talk to the others about coming to the game. I'd love to see you guys in the stands."

Marcelo is back. "Emmy, you have permission to go with Susan. I'm to take everyone else home."

With the word permission, I almost vault out of my chair. "Permission, huh? I'm not a puppy that he orders around."

Marcelo puts his hands in the air in surrender, "My words, not his. He said that if you feel safe with Susan, then that's fine with him."

"You know, you almost started World War III with that bad choice of words, Marcelo. I hope you will make better word choices before you speak next time. I'm not sure these girls could, or would, protect you." This advice came from Cecilia, for which I'm shocked but grateful.

I can't wait to get to Susan's car so we can talk. As we are walking, she pulls out a small tracker and shows me. I know this drill, stay quiet or at least take caution with what you say. I wonder if everyone keeps these little devices in their pockets?

Susan asks, "Are you good with directions to your place, or should I get out a map?"

"Oh, I know the way there. Are you planning to go to the game?" She smiles again, "Not sure about the game. I have to call into work and make sure they don't need me. When do you leave for the game? Are you driving?"

I hadn't thought about it. There has always been someone with me. I just say where I need to be and off we'd go. I need to be more independent. Time to take charge.

"I'm driving. Would you like for me to pick you up? I mean, if you can go. I haven't taken my Mustang out for a spin in days. It needs a little drive time."

I guess she's surprised because she wrinkles her brow. We arrive at her car and she pulls out an old mason jar with tissue in it and pushes the tracker into it, closing the lid tightly.

"Okay, we can talk now. It's behind its own window with a makeshift blanket around it. Hard to hear that way or so I'm told."

Relief fills me. "Yeah, I hate always having big brother listening. My apartment is just up here on the left. There are only eight units, so it is cozy. How far are you from here?"

Susan checks traffic and makes the left. "I can go tonight. I just didn't want to seem overeager. I'm not sure if it can hear us or not, but it is still tracking us, so I'm leaving it with you for now. Can't take it to my place, so just leave it in the jar."

I start to get out and she puts her hand on my arm.

"Marty's already here or I would go in and check the place out. Don't look at me crazy. I know because I can see his car and he's looking out the window. Plus, see the mailbox? There's a little gnome ornament hanging from it. He's there. He has my address."

"See you soon." I'm up and out of the car with my packages as I shout over my shoulder, "You have forty-five minutes, so be ready."

Fifty minutes later, I'm sitting in my Mustang outside Susan's place with Marty, go figure. I'm happy to be driving and trying to take some control over my life. Susan smiles, "Oh, I see you have your Bozo with you." If looks could kill, Susan would be dead. Marty never liked it when he was called a clown at the restaurant and it didn't work well now, either.

"So, you got the job of tagalong. That's my job, you know," Marty says with a sharp, biting tone.

"Well, you can't go everywhere I can," sings Susan.

This is going to be a long night if I can't stop this back and forth bantering. "Okay kiddies, it's time to play nice in the sandbox." I get two evil stares. I wonder which one will be the first to kick sand again. To my surprise, they both settle down and we have fun.

I'm dressed and waiting at the top of the tunnel to the basketball floor. Where are the cheerleaders? The team is here waiting for the signal to run in. Loyola's team is in front of us and their cheer squad in front of them. I hear the announcer introduce the Loyola team and coaches, and out they go. Just when I think I'm doing this entrance alone, the cheerleaders appear. I'm relieved and shocked to see Sterling, dressed in Mike's gear, standing next to me. Holy cow! Can he do this? Connie steps up and introduces Sterling as her new partner.

Sterling puts his hand on her shoulder, "We're on the same gymnastics team, so we sort of know each other."

"Oh, I knew that. Thank goodness he volunteered to help or my season would be over. Well, at least no stunts. He learned most this afternoon, so we should be good to go tonight."

I can hear the announcer and then the Cougar Brass starts up the fight song, our cue. I take off down the tunnel, take two steps in and begin my tumbling run across the floor followed by the cheer squad. The Houston Honey's have made a tunnel and are shaking their pom poms as the team passes. Our place on the sidelines is between the caged cougar mascot, Shasta and the Cougar Brass. We finish the fight song spectacle and wait as the team is introduced and the game starts. I am pleased to see Candy, my big sister in my sorority, approaching me with a giant red, helium-filled balloon. I am so glad she remembered. She ties it to the tail on my costume. It works great. It makes my tail stick straight out from my costume. Perfect. The crowd notices and seems to appreciate it, too.

I'm parading around, being careful not to get tangled with the cheerleaders or the band, or interfere with the game. I realize if I stand still, it blocks some of the fans' view so I keep moving. When I do stop, I pull it in tight so it is next to me. I notice that Shasta, the real cougar, is watching me from her cage. When I pass, I make sure to not slow down.

It's during a time out, as I'm coming back to the cheerleaders to perform a cheer at the sidelines, that I catch Sterling's eyes bugging out and I stop dead in my tracks. What's going on? What does he see? This hesitation gives Shasta the perfect opportunity she's looking for. I did not realize that every time I passed her cage, she would swing her paw out of the cage to try and get the balloon. I should have. The crowd would cheer and or boo as I passed her cage. I am so dumb for never looking behind me.

With the momentary pause, she catches the string and my tail, jerking me back against the cage. I feel her hot breath and low rumble while I'm pinned there. There is screaming from everywhere, including me. I bend my knees to try to launch away. Sterling has arrived at the same time the costume gives up. Sterling has both of my hands and pulls, so we both fly back and then slide in front of the cougar band. This amazing stunt is pulled off without my costume.

That is now in the cage with Shasta, who is making a quick kill and dinner of it. She's going to have a stomach problem later for sure. The balloon pops, making everyone hit the floor, even the teams. It sounded like a gunshot. Sterling is on top of me. Whistles blow. More chaos. Shasta's handlers are trying to retrieve what's left of my costume. The cheerleaders are checking on me. The teams have gone to their benches and the whole place becomes quiet.

The announcer comes on and makes a poor excuse for comic

relief. Things seem to settle. I'm handed a red uniform jacket from one of the Cougar Brass. I'm standing in just a sports bra, tights and ears. This jacket covers me, but just barely. I'm sure someday I will think this whole situation was funny, but for now I wonder how I managed to not peed my pants or end up as dinner for Shasta. It was scary!

The rest of the game is very normal and I can't wait for this day to end. On the way out of the stadium, it's all that is being talked about. A few people cut their eyes my way. Marty asks for my keys and I comply. This is the first time I've let someone drive my beautiful, midnight black, four on the floor, fastback 1970 Mustang. It is my pride and joy. I am looking forward to driving it home at the end of the semester in late May. Marty sees me hesitate.

"Emmy, I will be very careful with your toy. I understand your attachment to it. I feel the same about my cars."

I hand over the keys and smile. He does take care of his car and he isn't a crazy driver. I'm a little unnerved after my close encounter with Shasta. I'll never look at her the same.

THIRTY-FOUR

Houston OPS

- Kitten has five more regular games; two are home games. Sterling, Charlie and Susan will handle those.
- Continue to develop reports on the players in this group so we can determine who are leaders and who is just muscle.
- Should any have outstanding tickets or court appearances, HPD will pick them up and we'll do the interviews.
- We need further detail on the Houston Ratline its connection to the Mexican cartel.
- UH has spring break coming up in three weeks. Kitten is staying in town for now.

THIRTY-FIVE

Valentine Crazy

VALENTINE'S DAY CAN BE FUN, but for me it'll be a little crazy. Certainly awkward, to say the least. Marty might be my date this evening, but Charlie is who I want romantic alone time with. Charlie is not happy about this arrangement, but he understands.

Charlie seems different since he returned from his last assignment. He's quieter. He's listening. He's thinking. He's still romantic. There seems to be something wrong. I can't put my finger on it. This Valentine's party, or assignment, is weighing heavy on him. Our Valentine's Day will be February fifteenth, since the fourteenth is already taken with this. He says to not worry about the party, that it is necessary and we'll get along time together soon.

I would love to ask Marty if Charlie has said anything, but that might just complicate things. I think back to Caroline and all the many conversations we had about difficult times or emotions running around in our heads and wished for her wisdom. She always said I was a clear thinker. Well, except about myself. Caroline's sudden death in the car accident has made me depend on myself and that might not be so good. Right now is a good example.

I decide I need to seek advice, so I call Tootsie. She seems frustrated with something or maybe just impatient when she answers. Instead of launching into my thoughts and problems, I say, "Hey, you sound upset. Talk to me. I'm here for you." Thirty minutes later she takes a breath and now I'm sure my world, although weird, is not as stressful as hers. Between trying to teach Eddie's wife, Lu, English and a heavy load at college she has just discovered her longtime boyfriend. soon to be fiancé, is cheating on her. Yikes, that's a big load of craziness.

Tootsie, the ever-considerate friend, asks me about my Valentine's Day plans and I tell her what Charlie and I have planned. She starts in about her cheating boyfriend again and I ask her to give me the details of why she thinks that.

Her story is not really fact-based, more suspicion pieced together with second-hand accounts, but with no real evidence. I told her that and said, "He deserves the benefit of the doubt, just because you guys have so much history. Slow down, let him hang himself or save himself. Catch him in a lie that will start a conversation without you starting a fight. I mean, an innocent statement can get the ball rolling. Like, 'hey, Beth saw you downtown this morning. Wish I had known you were going. I would have liked to tag along.' Then shut up and let him hang himself, or save himself."

Tootsie sighs and says, "You're right. I was just embarrassed when Beth told me about it. I need to take a deep breath and give him a chance. I would want the same if the situation were reversed. Thanks, Emmy, for your clarity. I needed you. How did you know?" I hear noise in the background and she says she needs to go but will check in later. I say my goodbyes but she's gone before I finish. We have been on the phone for 30 minutes. My long-distance bill is going to be high. I need to cut back.

I'm dressed and ready to go, but I want Charlie to see this dress on me first, and alone, for a minute. He's here but hasn't answered me. I peek around the corner and he's alone on the sofa, on the phone.

When he sees me, his eyebrows rise, he stands and says to whoever is on the phone, "Gotta go, bye." It didn't sound like business, but his arms are around me and we are kissing before I can think of anything but him. He pushes me back and says, "Wow, this dress is made for you. I love it. What did the others say?"

I smile and tell him, "You are the first and most important review. Well, except for Susan in the dressing room but she doesn't count. Where will you be tonight?"

"I have paperwork from last month to finish, so I will be at the office but on call in case there is a need. I don't think that tonight will be a problem."

"It's a problem for me. I want you tonight." This comment earns another embrace and Charlie buries his face in my hair and takes a deep breath. He is breathing me in and it feels like he is losing something he wants to remember. He pushes gently back and looks at me, then we kiss again. So nice.

We are interrupted by a loud clearing of the throat from Sterling. He's dressed to party and I ask, "Where are you going?"

His eyes roll and a cute, sneaky smile comes out. "Well, if you must know, I have a date with Connie. You know, my new partner."

"Sounds like fun. Lucky you have no work tonight. I'm happy you boys get some downtime."

There's that sneaky smile again and I know he is up to no good. But he surprises me with, "Tonight, I'm mixing business with pleasure. Connie are I are having dinner at Ruth's Chris Steak House. She's delighted and, for that matter, so am I."

Marty steps in from the hall and adds, "It was difficult, but not impossible, to get him that reservation. This is the same place we're having dinner and our party. So, Susan and Sterling will be in the building, plus some of the work staff belong to us. There will be listening devices throughout, including the restrooms."

I turn to look at Marty. He is dressed in a lovely suit and so is Sterling. Two handsome studs. So much for a quiet moment with Charlie. "Wow, listening devices. Will both sides have them?"

Sterling comes back with, "Probably on them, but not planted in the restaurant. We have that covered. Tonight should be all party and no business. I hope so. Maybe I should test out my wishes on the boys."

I turn to go back to get my purse and realize all three are staring at me. "What?"

All three look uncomfortable and so I step up close to Charlie. "What am I missing? I've been around you three long enough to know there is something up. What gives?"

Charlie takes my hand and walks me away from Marty and Sterling. I look back and they have vanished. I mean gone.

"What's going on?"

Charlie steps in close, "Don't worry about them. Marty and Sterling know this evening is going to be a tough sell on your part. They are worried about you and the others working on this assignment. Tonight, everything hinges on how well you can act."

I pull my head back to look at him. He is stoic and silent. I sigh and say, "Do I need to drag out of you why, all of a sudden, this is more difficult than yesterday's shopping trip or the other night at the restaurant. I mean, I think they went as well as they could. I..."

Charlie's lips meet mine mid-word and he sits me down on the loveseat. I think he needs me to understand something that I haven't figured out yet. I can't stand this. "Charlie, what is going on? I can handle it. I trust you. We have been in tougher things together."

Charlie drags his hands through his hair and begins, "I know you can do this. You're a trooper. Marty is worried about tonight, but I'm not. Tonight, Marcelo is going to propose to Margarita, Ricardo to Cecilia, and Caesar to you. I know you will be ok with this because, like you said, we have been through worse. Marty is scared to death, so take it easy on him."

I reach over and hug him. There always seems to be another man between him and I. I have no words. I want to cry. If I cry, I will be a mess. Not only my makeup, but my emotions will let loose and I am not sure I'll be stable. I need to lock my emotions down, but I need to hold on to this man. Can I do both? Charlie holds me closer. We sit locked in each other's arms for, I guess, too long because I see Marty peek around the corner from the kitchen. He disappears, but the moment with Charlie is lost. He moves away from me.

As if that news wasn't enough, Charlie adds, "I've been worried about us. We seem to not get to just be. I hope this summer, when you are back in Washington, we can be a 'we' again."

I smile, "This summer you'll be in Washington? I mean, I

could only hope you might come for a while."

He smiles, "Yes, you've been telling the guys that you're going to drive your Mustang home from Houston. I've been assigned to go with you on this road trip. I have some business at Langley that will take two weeks, then I have some downtime. You and I get some together time, so chin up and let's get past tonight, the NCAA basketball playoffs, and your finals. Then, it's just us."

I look at him, lean in and whisper in his ear, "Oh, I'm going to find plenty of 'us' time between now and then. Maybe just small bits, here and there, but good ones." I try to be seductive but my wiggling eyebrows just make him burst into laughter. This laughter is taken as a sign that it is safe for Marty and Sterling to reappear.

I decide to not say a word to either of them about tonight's engagement party. I'm not trying to be mean, I just think Mr. Tall, Dark, and Handsome should be authentically nervous or, as Charlie said, "scared."

Truth be told, so am I now. "Ok guys, let's get this show on the road." I'm up and heading to the door. Sterling is following me. Marty hasn't moved. He keeps looking from Charlie to me and back. I look back, "What? Is something wrong?"

Charlie nods and Marty starts moving my way, "Okay, let's go."

The steak house is crowded and it smells wonderful inside. Sterling hasn't gotten here yet. I haven't figured out how they will end up at the party with us, but I'm sure it has all been planned out.

We are the last to arrive. Cecilia and Ricardo are greeting everyone and tell us they were worried something had happened. I take the blame, but Marty said he wanted to be fashionably late.

Our room has two tables, one with older couples at it and then our table of eight. Marcelo and Margarita, Mae and Miguel, Cecilia and Ricardo and us. The older couples are all family and friends but we have not been introduced, yet. It occurs to me that because Marty has spent time with Ricardo separately, he has likely met the men, at least.

Orders are taken, then the food arrives and after eating

everyone is just comfortably chatting. Ricardo turns to Marty and the other guys and says, "It's time to dance and share our surprise with the family." At this Marty, Miguel, Marcelo and Ricardo stand and, with the help of some wait staff, move a few pieces of furniture out of the way. Ricardo has music start and invites everyone to dance. All the older couples stand and move to the makeshift dance floor. One of my favorite songs starts playing. "Que Sera Sera" sung by Doris Day is such a classic and it is so poignant today. This is an easy, light song to dance to. For a moment, I drift away and forget my troubles. At the end of the song, Marcelo, Marty and Ricardo each bring a chair to the center and ask us to sit. Margarita, Cecilia and I sit as Ben E. King's 'Stand by Me' begins. This is it.

All three boys drop to one knee in front of us and ask, "Will you marry me?" Each has a ring box in hand, which they pop open as Ben says he won't be afraid. I stand, nodding vigorously, when I hear the words 'darling, stand by me.' I can see the relief in Marty. I move straight into his arms so there is no question of my answer. I breathe into his ear, "You did that perfectly." He kisses me on the cheek. "Thank you for making that easy." I can hear two very different reactions in the background. Margarita is screaming and sobbing, "Yes, yes, yes."

Cecilia gasped and said, "I've longed for this moment since the moment I met you." Everyone came back to the dance floor, even the older couples, for Frank Sinatra's 'The Best is Yet to Come.' This scene was written for a movie. We danced for a couple of more songs.

We are dancing close to the door of the private room when I see Sterling waving at me. I stop and point at my new ring, and gesture to Marty who it is.

Sterling walks over and shakes hands with Marty and then kisses me on the cheek. "Kitten, everyone is watching so make this good." Connie gasps, "That is a beautiful ring and a beautiful man to go with it." I nod, and Ricardo and Cecilia approach with Marcelo and Margarita on their heels. Marty introduces everyone and Ricardo invites them to join us.

Sterling has a camera and takes photos of all of us. He captures a few of the older couples in his background. I am sure this is so the team can identify all of them.

I rarely drink, so the two glasses of champagne have made me relaxed and I don't even notice the time passing. Marty leans in, "Kitten, it's time to go." We have danced all evening and I am ready to take my shoes off. New shoes are not the best to try to dance the night away in.

We say our goodbyes and I'm so relieved when we finally get to the car. Marty turns, "Emmy that went better than I thought it could. Thank you for making everyone believe it was real."

"Marty, it felt real. It could have been staged for a movie. I will always remember this night. So romantic. It was beautiful. Do you need this ring back?"

He looks surprised, "No, you will need it for a while."

My surprise must be written on my face, too. "Okay, I guess we will have to make some appearances here and there."

Marty rolls his eyes, "You have no idea. This group has a big family party planned. You and I are just small potatoes, but Ricardo's engagement is super big. It joins the two big families together and they plan on a huge party."

"Really, when?"

"Not sure, but sometime in May. Thank goodness it will be here in Texas and not in Mexico. When Ricardo first presented me with the idea, he wanted to fly to Mexico the next day and have a flashy party in her town. I knew that couldn't, and wouldn't, happen. I explained that your parents were not aware of how close we had gotten and I need to take it slow and not be in the news. I think your commitments here were considered and of course, Cecilia's finals. I also mentioned that I hadn't asked your parents and that would be tricky since they were in Washington. I think they want all the parents at the party, including yours. You and I traveling to Mexico before the summer, and me not being able to talk to them in person, is not just a problem but impossible."

All I could think to say was, "Oh."

Marty is talking but he is thinking on his feet and it is confusing. "Houston Ops is exploring all kinds of scenarios for this. I need to be tight with them to understand and track their power and you need to be safe. Both of these end games have problems. For now, we will use your commitments as a way to keep them at bay."

All I want right now is to climb into bed and cover my head. This is when I realize how difficult my parents' jobs are. And, for that matter, it's how the boys live, too. They have one foot in each world. This isn't easy. I'm hardly good at one world without trying to keep another one straight.

THIRTY-SIX

Houston OPS

- Kitten is going to Galveston with her sorority sisters. Our team will be in the house next door.
- Surveillance team will be all male so that interaction with Kitten's sorority sisters will not be suspicious. Agents Wells, Day and Kline already know many of them, so this should not be a problem.
- Ricardo's group will probably make an appearance. Check all rentals in a 5-mile radius and if any properties are owned by any family members of their group. There are to be no surprises.
- Kitten's parents are concerned that a member of the group will try to take her to Mexico.
- There is a block of tickets purchased for the play-off games by Ricardo's parents' business. We will have a team with them. Marty is going undercover as their guest.

THIRTY-SEVEN

Spring Break

WOW, SPRING BREAK IS JUST three weeks away and there are only two more home games. I'm sure no game will be as exciting as my last encounter with Shasta. I have two spare costumes, so I'm not worried about getting a costume in time, just keeping them clean. I'm pretty sure the Coogs will get an invite to the NCAA tournament.

The big surprise to me was that the sorority is renting a house in Galveston over the spring break week. I might get to go, depending on when and where the tournament is. I get the schedule tonight. Sterling and I will be there, for sure. My other concern is, when and where is this mega engagement party going to happen?

Houston is hosting the first round of tournaments at the Hofheinz Pavilion. The first game on Saturday is TCU and Notre Dame, with Notre Dame favored to win. We play New Mexico State as the second game of the day. All games will be televised. I'm excited to see how far we can go. The Coogs are ranked seventeenth in the nation going into the tournament. In our group is New Mexico State, Kansas, Drake, Texas Christian University, Notre Dame and West Kentucky State.

It was fun to help out since the Texan schools were considered hosts here in Houston. We all had jobs to do. I was assigned as a greeter, and to make sure all the mascots had what they needed for the televised games. I know the boys were around, but I was too busy to notice them. Ahhh, normal crazy life.

Our game against New Mexico is close, but we eventually

win. I am glad I helped with logistics in the days before because our cheerleading squad was prepared and looked good on TV, so my dad says. Our next tournament games are in three days. Notre Dame plays Drake and we will play Kansas. Notre Dame loses, and we go back and forth but lose in the last minute to a single basket. It was a heartbreaker. We will play Notre Dame for third place and Kansas will play Drake for the Midwest title with one team moving on to the final four.

The final four is scheduled for the Astrodome which is so exciting. The news people say it is the first time that a national championship is to be held in a domed stadium. I love being in the dome for football games, but I'm sure this will be so different. I will probably be on the meet and greet team again, which is good with me.

I had hoped I would get to spend some of the week at the beach house with my sorority and it looks like I can! Although it looks like the tournament is going to be keeping me busy, I can leave for two days. I'll drive to Galveston in the morning and will be back in time for the third-place game against Notre Dame. I get to party on St. Patrick's Day at the beach house after all! I need some fun in the sun.

THIRTY-EIGHT

Houston OPS

- The team at Hofheinz Pavilion is as usual. Agent Day will be with Kitten on arrival and Agent Wells is embedded as a cheerleader on her team.
- The beach house group is already in Galveston through the weekend.
- Marty, aka Caesar, will spend maximum time with Ricardo so he can establish a good rapport with the group. Marty is going to go to Mexico with the group after spring break and will be back before the end of April.
- The threat of someone kidnapping Kitten across the border is growing. Keep an eye or ear out for any communication about it.
- Working on security for the Final Four at the Astrodome. There will be many assets from across the country and our unit will be a small part of a big team. Your assignments are in your folders.

THIRTY-NINE

Beach House

I'M FINALLY FREE. MARTY IS coming later today with his new buddies, and I'm traveling with Charlie and Sterling. Because of the tournament, everyone's spring break plans have to be flexible. Charlie and Sterling have a pop-up camper on the back of Sterling's truck and he's following me to the beach house. My sisters said it's ok for them to park it on the property of the beach house. Candy, my big sister, thinks it is cool to have our private protection. Little does she know just how protective they are.

I was hoping to have alone time with Charlie, but that just doesn't seem possible. There are way too many eyes. Candy thinks I am juggling two men at once because she's seen me with Marty and Charlie. I can't explain. If I did, I'd not only put her in jeopardy, but it could also cause problems for the whole operation.

The beach house is on the Bolivar Peninsula. You take a free ferry from Galveston to it and then just drive right in to Crystal Beach. I can see the Greek letters, Phi Mu banner from the main road. The house is huge and I can see how we're all able to be here at once.

My room, if you want to call it that, is on the very top floor. It is the attic space turned into quasi-living quarters. It consists of a queen sized bed and an end table. There are two sets of windows up here. One is floor to ceiling and faces the water and the other is a porthole that faces the road. This space was clearly an afterthought to the design because it is not accessible from inside of the home. The outdoor stairs come up from the main floor deck. Most of the girls don't want this arrangement because you have to go out to the deck and then climb two floors up. At first I'm a little worried but after a suggestive look from Charlie, I realize how convenient this privacy will be.

Candy says, "I hope you don't mind being up so high. You don't drink, so navigating the stairs safely shouldn't cause you trouble."

I smile knowingly. "I'm happy for the quiet up here and the sunrise will be picture perfect."

Sterling hands Candy a nice bottle of red wine with a wink, "Here is a thank you for the parking place. I know you are old enough to enjoy it."

Candy loves wine so she beams and thanks him. I open the sliding glass door to the small private deck and just breathe in the sea air. "I needed this," I sigh contentedly.

Sterling left with Candy, so Charlie steps in close, puts his arms around me and pulls me tight. "Well, I needed this." He kisses the back of my neck. I lean back into him and allow all my muscles to relax. I turn to kiss him back and he pulls me back inside. I know what I want and so does he. He locks the door and within minutes we are naked on the bed, touching and kissing and curled in each other's arms.

I don't know how long we were alone but it was just what I needed. Sterling warns us of Marty's approach by shouting a greeting as he and Ricardo approach the house. I'm dressed and down the stairs to join in with a greeting of my own. Time to play the game again. I clamber down to the ground floor to meet up with the two of them. I act surprised that they have come by the beach and not in a car. We walk back toward the beach which, I realize, is Marty's way of showing me, and Sterling and Charlie, where he is staying.

Ricardo laughs, "It is quicker to walk. We are just there where the flags are hanging over the deck."

I look where he is pointing, but there are many houses with flags. "Which flags?"

Marty leans in intimately and whispers, "Be careful to recite what I am about to say so the team can hear." Then he raises his volume a little, enough for Ricardo to hear but still be considered between us, "Mi amor, it's the blue one with the Mexican, Spanish, Italian and American flag on the corners of the deck."

I smile and nod, "Yes, I think I see it. It's dark blue with a deck painted white."

I look up at him and move in closer. "I know the American flag above the door, but is that the Spanish flag on the far corner and the Italian flag closest to us and then that must be the Mexican flag in the middle? Let's see, it's the... one, two, three, four... fifth house from us. You're right, it's much closer to walk to."

Marty smiles, pleased how I relayed that to the team. I turn to Ricardo and ask, "Did everyone come with you... The girls, I mean?"

Ricardo is looking over my head at the house I just came from. I turn to see what has his attention. He speaks but his eyes are still on the house. "The girls will come later with Marcelo. For now, it is just the two of us. Who are you staying with? And how long?"

All seven of the girls are standing at the rail, plus Sterling. I look back at Marty, then to Ricardo. "My sorority rented this for the week. Those are my sorority sisters, plus Sterling. He is staying in his camper parked over there. Why?"

"Oh, no reason. Lots of nice eye candy up there. Who is the tall blonde? She looks familiar."

I sort of laugh which causes him to take his eyes off her. "That's Kaye. She was in playboy a couple months ago. They did an article on the Homecoming queens from all the football conferences. Kaye is the reigning Miss Southwest Conference. Now I know what you have been reading."

He frowns, then smiles. "Ah, but I know this girl differently. I remember her now. She was at a party I was at and she certainly is a party all on her own. Do you party like her?"

I'm pissed her reputation is rubbing off on me and I don't like it. Ever since the restaurant adventure with Jim, I've shied away from her. "No, she is her own person and I don't know her well. Do you want to meet her? I am not sure Cecilia would like it, but I can call her down here."

Marty slowly shakes his head, "We don't have time right now. We have to pick up the food for tonight. Maybe later. We've planned a bonfire on the beach. We just came to check on you. I will be back for you later."

"Okay, what time will you be back?" I want a timeline so I can get some sun before then.

"Is there a phone in the house? I can call you ahead of time." As he says this, he comes in close and kisses me.

I'm not sure of the number, but a quick shout gets an answer. Ricardo and Marty are on their way back to their beach house.

"Hey guys, is the party a private one?" I shout at their backs.

Ricardo turns and shares a sneaky smile, "it's a beach party, so open to anyone on the beach. Tell your eye candy to come on over. There will be plenty to eat and drink."

Marty blows me a kiss and I can almost hear the girls above really weighing the two men I have on the hook; Marty heading down the beach and Charlie standing near them on the balcony. I don't have an explanation, at least not one I can tell.

The rest of the day revolves around me, the beach, a good book, and Charlie and Sterling by my side. I shower and dress early, which leaves me waiting on the deck for Marty's call. Charlie is not coming to the bonfire, but Sterling and Bob will be there plus others. I'll know who are the good guys because all the men will offer to get me a drink and the women will wink at me. I'll always look at people in a crowd differently from now on. I wonder how many events I have been to where other things were happening just under the surface. I think many and I was just oblivious.

As much as I worried about the bonfire, it's so much fun. There's a giant bonfire about fifty feet from the outdoor shower, at the end of the walkway from the house to the beach. There are logs to sit on around the fire. Ricardo seems to have thought of everything. Over by the piles of food, you can find anything you could ever think of to drink, from alcohol to soft drinks. The food is fried chicken, corn on the cob and beans. I have never been to such a fancy beach party. There are beach blankets, chairs and even a makeshift dance floor with lights strung around so you can see the volleyball players without falling into them. He's arranged a picture-perfect evening, something you'd see on a movie set.

Everyone is happy, dancing and just enjoying the beautiful spring night. Cecilia, Mae and Margarita, plus a few girls I haven't met, are here, along with all my sorority sisters plus the security detail assigned to this. They're all mingling happily. Marty and I sit to the side for a while, alone, and he explains what was going on from his side.

"Emmy, it's going to get a little crazy in the next few weeks. I need you to be careful. Being alone with any of these people could get you taken. I will be around, but Ricardo thinks I am too worried about what your parents will think and, as he says, "It's not manly." After the tournament next week, I will go with him to Mexico and be back in mid-April. The big party is on April twentieth, at the River Oaks Country Club, I think. What other things would you have going on besides class?"

I'm glad we're talking about business. "I have class, finals, and socially I am in charge of Sigma Chi Derby week. Then there's the drive home around the twenty-first of May."

He turns and scrunches his nose at me. He's seriously so cute when he does that. "What the hell is Derby Week?"

I guess it does sound weird to outsiders. My dad was a Sigma Chi and I have seen pictures of him in his derby. I think it was much more dignified then. He is still looking at me all scrunched up. "Okay, let's see. Where do I begin so it doesn't sound so silly?"

"Too late for that, just cut to the chase. We might be interrupted any minute. I am going to kiss you because I think Margarita is thinking about coming over here. Maybe she will stay away if she thinks she is bothering us."

He does kiss me and his hands are roaming all over. It probably looks to her like we are getting ready to get busy. I look over his shoulder. "She's gone. Okay, back to the derby thing. All the participants decorate the derby hat they are given. Some derbies are worth more than others. I'm decorating mine as a Phi Mu and the cougar mascot, but I'm also decorating three other sports guys derbies. The object is to steal the derby and keep it for ransom. The more popular the person, the more it is worth in ransom. One of my guys is Rob Hall from the basketball team, and another is Robert Newhouse from the football team. Oh, and some golfer dude who won the Walker Cup and has been to the Masters as an amateur. I think his name is Doug Ballentine. All of them will wear their derby on campus. If it's stolen, then to get it back money is exchanged and is given to Sigma Chi's philanthropy, their designated charity."

Marty shakes his head and stands, then we walk closer to the water. There are others on the beach enjoying each other in very intimate ways. We continue to walk back toward my place. Marty is asking me lots of questions about when, where, and how long this derby thing is. I've already told Charlie all about it. It's on-campus only and not in your car or dorm. You can steal the person and the derby, or just the hat, it doesn't matter. It's all in fun and for charity.

Marty stops, "Can anyone steal you and your derby, or does it have to be a fraternity member? Where do they take you if they steal you? I'd like to put a tracker in your derby and on you."

I am so stunned that he sees this as a threat. "You really think someone will use this as a way to take me? It's just a fraternity tradition." As I am saying this out loud, I realize this could be the perfect cover for a kidnapping. Wow.

As we get to the stairs that lead up to the house, Marty stops and kisses me, then turns to leave. "Yes, it's a big possibility but you'll be watched by everyone."

As I walk up the stairs, I think I'm here alone but I feel a presence. I don't see anyone, but I can feel it. This feeling, plus what Marty has just said, has me more than on edge. I turn the corner as I get to the top and a figure comes toward me. I start to turn and run.

"Emmy! Wait, it's me." The figure is close enough to see that it's my dad. I hug him and then bombard him with questions.

"How? Why…? Is mom okay?" He hugs me back and all is well when I'm in my daddy's arms. I feel safe.

"Everyone is fine. I'm here to check on you and tell you we are aware of your assignment. Mom and I are not happy you're pulled in again. It is a prime example of how one thing can take a wrong turn and you just can't stop it. The Houston team is all over this. Just listen and be safe."

I hug him again and promise I'm being as careful as I can and trying my best to do as I am told. We stand there in the dark and quiet, with only the noise and light from the bonfire down the beach for a long time. It's nice to just be in the moment. Dad finally turns and kisses me on the forehead, "I can't stay or be seen here. Got to go. We love you." I blink and he is gone.

Did I just dream that or was he here? Right when I've convinced myself he was a ghost, I see him walking with two other people on the beach, away from the bonfire. My superhero.

FORTY

Houston OPS

- Whitey successfully spent time with Kitten in private. He was grateful for the effort.
- Beach time went well… Good work all around.
- Tournament security is complicated and multiple agencies are involved. Check your folders daily for your assignments and any changes will be on the big board.
- Yellow badges are for assets and all have embedded trackers.
- Green badges are us, the security.

FORTY-ONE

Astrodome

THE ASTRODOME IS AN AMAZING place. I've been there many times for football games but as of now, I've never come in from the regular gates. From the field, the view is breathtaking. We enter the game from one of the on-ramps and as I run in, I always feel so small in a giant world. The news media call it "the eighth wonder of the world," and I agree.

Today, we are here helping the cheer squads from the four competing schools get acclimated to the place. The look on their faces is just like mine the first time I came... Just wonderment and awe. I'm helping the UCLA team to their lockers and then onto the field. For this tournament, it's not actually a field; it has an elevated floor for the game. The astroturf has been removed and seats are set up closer, plus there's an open area so you can see from the regular seats. The dome has big screens that the game will be played on for the fans wanting to see the game better. I'm sure this will be a Texas-sized spectacle.

Security is tight. We all have badges around our necks. Mine's a different color than the others and I want to ask Charlie why. It also seems thicker. I didn't even notice either difference until one of the UCLA cheerleaders mentioned we both had badges the same color. I must have looked funny at him because he leaned in and asked, "Who are you?" I still looked at him kind of crazy.

Silly me, I answer, "I'm Emmy, the cougar mascot for the University of Houston."

The girl standing next to him giggles and says, "I'm so glad you said your name again, I'd forgotten."

I tried to smile at this ditsy girl and nod, but he just looked at her like he was embarrassed for her. "Uh, Katie, her name's on her tag. I'm John." He leaned in and whispered, "My dad's in politics so when I travel I'm tagged, too, just like you. It sucks sometimes. So, who are you?"

Is this guy for real? I'm just about to answer when Charlie appears from nowhere and grabs my hand. "She's taken so keep your Californian paws off her." I hadn't realized he had his hand on my arm and was still invading my personal space.

John took a small step back and straightened up, "I'm just comparing badges. We have the same color."

Charlie steps around me and comes in close, "That badge gets you protection and so does hers, but mine makes me the protector. Got it?"

I step in close to both, they look like bandy roosters ready to fight. "I'm just fine and need to do my job. It really doesn't matter who I am."

John sort of pushes at Katie to move, "Come on, let's get this done. We have practice back at your university's gym." With that, John walked away only to turn back to me. "Are you coming?"

I follow, answering him and Charlie at once. "Yes, I'm coming and I will see that you get transportation back to campus. Charlie, can you check on our ride?"

Everyone seems to be on edge. I try to put that on the back burner but I can see that John is still simmering. He sits on the edge of the newly erected basketball court and I sit next to him. "Hey, look, I'm really no one that important but Charlie and I are an item, so he gets a little possessive. My name is Emmy McCormick. It won't likely be recognizable to the public, nor will my parent's names. I'm an asset because, if compromised, it could hamper their jobs. I'm sorry about Charlie."

He cuts his eyes at me, "It's okay. I was just excited to meet someone who is watched like me and seems normal. Other kids, teens or whatever, are so screwed up by all the privileges. You are a breath of fresh air and it makes me realize that maybe someday I'll make it past this overprotected time."

He turns his whole body to me and sticks out his hand for a handshake. "Hi, I'm John. Let's call a truce."

I shake, "No truce needed. There was never a war, just a very small skirmish."

When we arrive back at campus, John says his goodbyes and the cheer team thanks me. I give them their schedule for game day and excuse myself to the car waiting on the curb for me. I heard Katie ask, "Who is she? I mean, she even has a driver." I didn't hear John's answer.

Meeting John made me realize there are others in the same boat as me and it's not easy for them either.

Game day is exciting and fast-paced. After everyone is in and the teams make their entrances, the games begin. I am in the mezzanine section with the other students who were guides. Both games are fun and it's a long day. West Kentucky fell to Villanova and Kansas fell to UCLA. The national champion will be either Villanova or UCLA.

March twenty-seventh is more than a busy day. I can't seem to find my ride to the dome. I call Sterling and no answer. I guess he's already left, and really it's supposed to be Marty picking me up, but he didn't answer either. I'm at the gym and it's crazy busy. John stops and I wish him good luck. He asks where my ride is and I explain I don't know.

His next words surprise me, "I guess you were forgotten in the crowd. Let's mess with them a little. Come on the bus with us to the dome. When you get there with us, it will be clear that someone slipped up. It's good, every once in a while, for them to see their mistakes. It keeps them on their toes." I can see his point, and I don't want to drive my car, so I jump on the bus.

Bob, my new friend/agent from the restaurant, is at the security gate and just stops dead when he sees me with the UCLA cheer squad and their band. As I show my badge and step through, he's on me, asking a ton of questions. "Where is Marty? Why aren't you with him? What happened?"

I put a finger to his lips, "First, I'm with them," waving my hand at the group, "because I was forgotten. Second, I have no idea what happened. And third, I thought Marty was to get me at the gym but he didn't show. So, settle down. Today it seems like security needs security. Make your call, report in."

John waves and continues on and I wait with Bob. Charlie arrives and we move away from the gate. "Okay, something's up. Marty was supposed to pick you up. He has tickets in the real seats for you and his new gang to watch the big game. We are checking on him through Mae as we speak. Come with us."

Okay, now I'm worried about Marty. Bob pats me on the back, "Good that you came with the UCLA group or we wouldn't have known."

What started as a desire to teach these boys a lesson about leaving me behind, went to serious concern about Marty. He's so careful, I know something is wrong. We've gone upstairs and down many halls. Together, we enter a noisy room with lots of chatter and busy people. Charlie asks out loud, "Any intel on Marty?"

This got him lots of stares and head shaking. As we turn to go, we hear, "Hey wait, I got something." An older man with grey sideburns who I've never met before comes close. "Mae finally answered and she says Ricardo changed plans and took Marty with him in his car and sent Marcelo to pick up Emmy. Mae was upset because Marcelo isn't scheduled to go to the game. She thought if Marcelo picked up Emmy, those two would have been on their way to Mexico by way of a private plane. Ricardo and Marty are leaving tomorrow for Guadalajara. I assured Mae that Emmy is here with us and that we'll take it from here. That settled her down a little."

I'm looking at everyone and no one, just thinking. I get this angry idea. "So, boys, if this had happened in 'real life,' I would be angry at Marty and I would know how to get into the stadium through the team entrance. I'd find him in the stands and be so angry that he forgot me. I can just be the normal girlfriend/fiancé that got left behind. Marty is smart, he will apologize and walk away with me to calm me down."

Charlie smiles, "That would work. Just be careful. Do we have eyes on their seats? Is he there? She can't go there until he's there."

He gets a rapid response. "Yes, eyes on the seats. No, he's not seated yet. He's in the building. Look, there he is in with

Ricardo and his group." Everyone eyes the screen. It's grainy but it is Marty and Ricardo, plus Mae and Cecilia. I can't tell who the others are.

I squeeze Charlie's hand. "I guess I'm up. I need to know how to get there safely. I don't want one of the others to intercept me. Sterling is here helping, isn't he? He could escort me."

"I sure can. I came as soon as I got word there was a problem. Let's go and get this show back on the road." All turn to see Sterling in the doorway.

He strides towards me and I high five him, "Perfect timing! I'm as ready as I can be."

Charlie is by my side and furrows his brow, "You do realize that Ricardo's man just tried to kidnap you, according to Mae. Stay in a public area. If you must go to the restroom, make Mae go with you. She may not break cover, but she at least will stay with you until help arrives. In her opinion, you complicate things."

I can see his point and kiss him on the cheek. "Yes, sir, I will stay in plain sight. Thanks, everyone here, for your eyes and ears on me."

Sterling and I slip out of the control room and head to an elevator to get us down to the mezzanine floor. Then, a quick walk around to the entrance to the correct section. I put on my angry face and head down to the field and then over to the newly built floor on the field. I show my badge to get to the field area and can see the back of Marty and Ricardo's heads. I guess someone has alerted them because before I can get to them, they both turn and stare. I stop dead and wait. I can see Marty talking to Ricardo. Marty starts towards me. I fold my arms across my chest. tap my foot and try to project steam out of my ears. He's moving fast. One of the guys with them starts to follow and it looks like Marty chastises him. The guy looks at Ricardo and, at Ricardo's nod, retreats.

Marty tries to hug me when he is close and I push him away. He grabs my arm and says through gritted teeth, "Good show, keep it up. Struggle a little. Then slap me when I try to kiss you. Let this play out for a minute then give in. We'll walk away." I do and he does try to kiss me. When I slap him, I hear a gasp from close by and an usher comes up to ask if I'm okay. I smile and notice his green badge. "I'm good. We'll be back after I get something to drink and an explanation." He nods and opens the gate to the steps that lead to the refreshment area.

A few minutes later, with a drink in hand, Marty has me up against the wall and is towering over me. "Okay, do you see anyone too close to us?" I shake my head. "I am so glad you are okay. How did you get away from Marcelo? How did you get here? This morning spiraled out of control."

I answer all his questions and tell him about the control room visit. Then I reach up and run my hand over where I slapped him. I've never slapped anyone before and I left a mark. "Are you okay?"

He nods, "Not the first time a woman has slapped me and won't be the last. I'm just fine. You do hit hard though."

With a chuckle, I lean in and tell him, "Marcelo is approaching. Get ready for me to get mad again."

He brushes his finger against my lips and says, "No, me first." He turns and shouts, "What the hell, man? You were given one, simple task. This lovely lady had to get a ride with the UCLA band and cheer squad. That is not safe. If this wasn't a public place, I'd show you a thing or two."

Marcelo backs up realizing Marty is about to explode. This was my opening. "This lack of planning could have had serious consequences with my dad if something had happened. I was lucky that the group had not left yet. Come on Marty, the game is about to begin. I'm not leaving your side."

Marcelo follows us back to the seats. When we arrive and are greeted by everyone, I cling to Marty. Ricardo points to a seat with the girls for me, but Marty shakes his head. "She's not leaving my side. I won't lose her this way."

Ricardo blows out a breath and gets everyone to move down one to free up a seat next to Marty, keeping Marty next to him.

I like basketball and I get into the game like everyone else. The early game saw Western Kentucky beat Kansas, taking the third-place spot. This game has been back and forth. UCLA does prevail and the place goes crazy. It's at this moment that I get frightened. I jump up with the others to cheer but I hang on to Marty the entire time. This would be the perfect time to get separated. Not a good idea. Ricardo leans in and says, "Marty, let's go. Emmy can ride with the girls."

Marty holds on tighter to me, "No, I'll ride with the girls then, too. Not letting my sweet thing out of my sight. What restaurant are we heading to? I think I heard you say 'Ninfa's' on Westheimer."

Ricardo snaps his fingers and one of the guys says to me, "Take my place in Ricardo's car. I will escort the other beautiful women."

FORTY-TWO

Houston OPS

- The tournament went well. Most assets on their way home and safe so far.
- Close call with Kitten ... We have to rethink relying on Agent Wells for security while he is undercover.
- Kitten's commitment to Derby Days on campus is in your folders. Check for your part, this should be a straightforward event.
- Several assets from the tournament are staying in town for a couple of days, so we will still be on call.

FORTY-THREE

Sorority and Derby Days

AFTER A TRIP TO THE craft store, raiding my art supplies, and hours of work, I have all four derby hats completed. Charlie is just sitting there, trying to keep the glitter off of himself. "I can't be seen with all the glitter attached everywhere."

I try to ignore his so-called glitter problem. "Today is when I present them to their owners and make sure I get a photo with them and their hat. I asked them all to come by the Cougar Den at the University Center around one. All the other decorated derbies will be there to be given out, too. I am sure the 'Daily Cougar' will be there to get photos."

Charlie rolls his eyes at me. "I hope, when we go outside, this windy day will help me get rid of this shiny crap. I feel like I fell into a bowl of it and wallowed around in it like a pig in the mud."

I have boxes ready to put each one in so they will be a surprise to each one of the guys.

I am not sure Charlie is even interested in seeing my derbies, but I decide to show him my creations anyway. Before I can start, Sterling arrives. "Hey, do you two know you have sparkly stuff everywhere? Oh, Charlie! I love how you look, so sparkly. It suits you."

A pillow flew by me and Sterling easily dodged it. Sterling pretend shouts from the other side of the room, "did you make mine and my tennis team girl, too?"

"Yes, they are in the box over there and if you take them out in here, you will be sparkly, too."

Braver now, Sterling steps closer. "Are mine as cool as these?"

"I'm just about to tell Charlie all about them as I pack them to travel. Yours are similar, so look and listen so you will not be so surprised when you see yours. My derby is this one. It has the Phi Mu Greek letters and the words written out on one side and a painted cougar on the other with cougar ears attached. I have used so much pink and red glitter, it's heavy."

Charlie interrupts, "What's with the pink? I thought that the school colors are red, white, and black."

I impatiently continue, "Red for the University of Houston and pink for my sorority." I place it in the box and close the lid.

"Then, the golfer's derby is simple. It has the cougar logo painted on the left side like mine, his name on the back, a golf ball painted on the front with Houston on the right side. I used red glitter on the word Houston and outlined the golf ball with silver glitter. I only put his first name, Doug, on it because his last is so long."

Sterling smiles and nods, "I like it."

I put his in its box and continue. "On Rob Hall's derby, I painted it basketball orange on top with the telltale black lines. I like this one. On top of the basketball, I put his name and number and, of course, the U of H logo in red glitter. What do you think?"

Charlie is still trying to de-glitter himself but answers me. "It's better than the pink everywhere. I might wear those last two."

"Well, if you look carefully, you can see my signature in pink and Phi Mu in Greek letters on them. I had to sign them." I enjoy this kind of stuff. It feeds my artistic side.

Sterling is opening the box with his inside. "Mine is so cool! I won't take it out, but I can see the signature. Why do they all have Sigma Chi on them?"

This time I roll my eyes at them. "It's the Sigma Chi's Derby, duh. This last one is for Robert Newhouse. He is my assigned football player. His is like the basketball hat, but instead it has a football painted on it. Name, number, and enough glitter to make it noticeable."

Sterling is helping me get them all in boxes with lids on them.

"Emmy, is there a prize for the best-decorated derby?"

"Yep, there's a little trophy. You also get to be in the front for the water balloon race. I'm not the fastest, so that'd be good for me. There are lots of people decorating derbies so there's no guarantee that I will win."

With that, we head out with all the boxes packed. To Charlie's delight, we step out and are almost immediately windblown and glitter-free, mostly. We head out to the University Center and the Cougar Den for lunch and then the presentation of hats. I am wearing my Cougar costume and Sterling is in his cheer duds. It is seriously busy here.

We find a table, get lunch and just enjoy the chaos. After lunch, I set my boxes of hats on the Phi Mu table and await instructions from the Sigma Chi president. After the mics are set up and the hats are displayed, the presentations begin and go on and on. I know it is important to give each sport it's due, but it is two hours of meet and greets. Thankfully, all the events are on Saturday, not today. I'm exhausted. Too many hours working on the derbies mean I need some real sleep before all the events begin.

I am entered in only two events, the water balloon race and, of course, the derby steal. The balloon race is Saturday and just one of five events on Saturday. The tug of war is the dirtiest, the raw egg race is messy, too, so the water balloon race seemed safest to me. Well, there is the hairy chest contest, but I don't qualify for that.

The derby steal is all week but there are only a few hours that your derby can be stolen. You are not allowed to hide during that time. You cannot be in class when it is stolen. Most of the steals happen on your walk to and from class. I've taken to walking/running from building to building. So far, I've only had one close call. It was coming out of the College of Education building and the next closest building is a good sprint. Thank goodness, my pursuer is slower than me. I know this event is driving Charlie and Sterling a little crazy.

It is Saturday morning and I've finished the balloon race. It's the last time our derbies can be stolen. Of the seventy or so that started the week, it looks like there are about twenty-five here at the starting line. I am sure this is where I will lose mine, but I'm going to give it my all.

The starting line is at the Newspaper office we have to make it to the University Center. Once you make it to the sidewalk in front, you're safe. I try to stay in the middle of the exploding group of bodies heading out the door. I can see that this is not going to be easy. I think I'm going to go right and head down the walk toward Shasta's area in the trees between the dorms and the University Center. It is a little longer but the trees provide some shelter. Several others go that way with me. I can see Cecilia, Margarita, and Mae in the distance cheering me on. I'm not even thinking of stopping to talk so I wave as I get closer. There are people everywhere. Some are cheering, some are screaming as their derby is stolen and some, like me, are trying to escape silently. Mae is signaling me to go left, but Cecelia and Margarita are beckoning me to come close to them. To my left is a large group looking for victims to catch. I choose to come close to the girls. Mae looks furious. Does she want me caught? Cecilia signals for me to hide behind them. I think this is a great idea, it's like moving cover and I should be able to sprint to the finish line at the end of the tree line.

My moving cover, aka the girls, and I get to the densest part of this stand of trees when my world changes again. My derby is snatched from my head and I am grabbed from behind all at once. I start to add to the screaming around me with my screams when a white cloth covers my nose. In my ear, I hear, "This time, I have you. Sleep for a while so I can deliver you to the boss." If he said more I don't remember because I'm out.

FORTY-FOUR

Houston OPS

- Kitten is missing. She left the race starting point but didn't make it to the finish line.
- She was spotted with others, going into the trees between her old dorm and the university center, close to Shasta's habitat.
- Cecilia, Margarita, and Mae were seen on campus.
- Her hat had a tracker, so where is it? Does she have one?
- Answers, we need answers!

FORTY-FIVE

Snatched Again

MY BRAIN IS SWIMMING. I feel sick. I know you can be kidnapped with your derby and I would have surrendered if caught, but drugging me is not part of the rules. This feels wrong. I'm going to pretend to be asleep and listen. Talking. There's talking.

Who is this? I feel like I know these voices. "She won't be out much longer. Where is the pickup car?" That's Marcelo.

"Why didn't you let me at least ask her to come with us?" That's Cecilia.

"Did you hurt her when she fell? Caesar and Ricardo will kill you if you did." And that's Margarita.

"I don't care where the pickup car is, we need to keep moving. People will come looking for her and anyone else who doesn't make it to the finish line. Where is the damn hat? If it doesn't make it to the finish line, then a whole lot of people will be looking for her and the hat."

That's Mae. Marcelo is whisper shouting in her face, and sadly mine, too, because I'm propped up next to her. "Shut up, bitch! I have this under control and I don't need your help."

With that, Mae is on her feet and I'm on the ground. She realizes her mistake and comes to the ground next to me but, too late. I hit hard and there's a bleeding gash chin. Can I stay quiet? Mae is cradling me and is wrapping something around my head. She shoos the other girls away. "I have this under control, just get us out of here."

My head is pounding and I'm still present but I know I am

bleeding and I want to touch it. I stir a little and Mae whispers in my ear. "Stay still, you'll be ok. Marty should be back from Guadalajara today, which is where I expect we are going."

I guess the car arrives and I'm hoisted inside it. I open my eyes just long enough to see my derby on the ground where we were sitting. What now? Do I depend on Mae? Do I hope that Marty is there, wherever there is? Marty was so sure the party would be in May. He was sure it would be a day or two after finals. Why are they taking me, and where?

I succumb to some sort of sleep or daze, only to be roused as we stop in a driveway of a huge house. This looks like a very expensive neighborhood. My dad's words echo in my pounding head. "Fight or flight," which is best here? I can see through my lashes that the long driveway has a gate and it is closing. No escape there. I can feel people all around me. So, I'm not going to win a fight just yet. I have kidnapped before so I decide to be the injured, unconscious body for a little while longer.

There are angry, hushed voices all around. I am moved from the car to the house, up some stairs and on to a bed. Someone is removing the scarf from my head and I hear an intake of breath followed by rapid Spanish.

"Ella necesitará puntos de sutura y tendrá que ser un cirujano plástico o no cicatrizara bueno. Limpia la herida y haré la llamada."

The doctor-like person moves away and gentler hands, probably a woman, starts to clean my face. She is close and whispers in English, "I know you're awake. They're all gone. You can talk to me. I won't hurt you. You need stitches, so they went to call for a plastic surgeon."

Should I trust this voice? I want to cry. I need a plastic surgeon, that's bad. I try to look at her through my lashes. She has turned her face to reach for something. I have never seen her before. She continues to clean my face and whispers again.

"Kitten, I am on your side of this. I am undercover like your Marty, uh Caesar. I cannot do much for now, but I can alert the right people soon. I am off duty in an hour. I'm one of the housekeepers here. I have some nursing experience, so that is why I'm with you."

If this is a trick, it is a good one. I slowly open my eyes and take her in. She is youngish and Hispanic. She smiles. I try to turn my head but it hurts. She leans in like she is cleaning but she isn't even touching my skin. "There is a guard at the door, so don't talk too loud. Marty should arrive any moment now. Be careful. Trust no one."

I nod, but in my head I keep thinking about 'trust no one'. I should check out my surroundings and plan my escape. I try to sit up. This isn't working. I should wait for Marty. I'm scared and I don't want to be here. What do they want? How did this happen again? I have escaped before, but I don't know if I can do it again. This is not like the ranch where I was held by the real Caesar. This is a well-maintained, wealthy, fully-staffed home. I want to speak but my face hurts.

I give myself a mental slap. If no one but this person is here for you then suck it up and use her help. Trust, but be wary. I know talking is going to hurt. I rush the words out through almost unmoving lips. "I need a drink. What's your name? Help me sit up."

She looks over her shoulder at the guard. He is looking at us. "The girl needs a drink and I need to sit her up. Can you help?" He hesitates then comes close and helps sit me up. My head spins as I am moved but I don't throw up. Thank God for small miracles. As soon as I am upright, he returns to his chair by the door.

"My name is Carmen." She hands me a cup with a straw. I try to drink but she says, "Stop. Using the straw is making your wound bleed. Try taking a small sip from the cup." I can see over the cup that the guard is watching closely.

Carmen speaks softly, just for me again. "The doctor has given you a shot to make you sleep. Try not to fight it. I'm not leaving until I know your Caesar is back. I will just sit here with you, even though my work time is over in an hour. He should hopefully be back before then." If she said more, I didn't hear it. I slept.

I awoke to a lot of angry men's voices and some seriously intense pain. One voice, thankfully, was Marty's. The pain brought my mind back to the new reality of being a captive. He is shouting at Ricardo as he bursts in the door. Carmen and the guard are on their feet as he rushes towards me.

Marty practically yells over his shoulder in Spanish, "Oh mierda. Qué le has hecho a ella? Quiero una explicación y, donde está el doctor?

Marty scoops me into his arms and I hurt, but having him this close is a luxury that I melt into. I look up to see him wink at Carmen. "Quien es esta mujer? Ella es una enfermera? He still is talking in a raised voice and she takes a step back and speaks in Spanish to him.

"Si, señor Caesar, soy enfermera pero no estoy registrada en los Estados Unidos. Soy de Panama." This, I understand. She's a nurse, but not registered in the States. She's from Panama.

I try to speak. "Mi amor, she has been kind. I like her."

This slight movement causes a small trickle of blood to slide down my chin. This, I can see, freaks him out. He is moving toward the door with me in his arms and Carmen is following close. "I'm taking her to the hospital."

Ricardo speaks for the first time. "Tengo un cirujano plastico en camino para cuidarla. El medico inicial parecio pensar que era lo mejor. Tenemos una pequena enfermeria en el pasillo donde la atenderan tan pronto como llegue."

Marty keeps moving and the guard steps out of his way. "Emmy, Ricardo has a plastic surgeon on the way. Apparently, the initial doctor seemed to think that was best. I'm taking you with me until the plastic surgeon arrives, so please don't talk. It makes you bleed. Carmen can come with us for now."

He is face to face with Ricardo, "Hasta entonces, ella estara en mi havitacion conmigo. Si quieres que esta enfermera este alli, esta bien conmigo." He pushes by Ricardo and strides purposely down the hall to another door. Carmen has moved past him to open the door for him. He nods and steps inside to a lovely bedroom. He sits me on the bed and turns to Ricardo who is now standing in the doorway, "Cuanto tiempo antes de que el cirujano este aqui?" He asks how long until the surgeon arrives.

Marty walks towards Ricardo. Ricardo looks past his shoulder at me but answers Marty, "Pronto deberia ser cualquier minuto." Any minute, he replies.

Marty is seething at this point and says in a measured voice full of anger, "I told you I would bring her here. This was not necessary. She has been injured because of your carelessness."

There is commotion behind Ricardo and fast words in Spanish that I could not hear. Ricardo turns to Carmen. "El doctor ha llegado. Vas a ayudar y preparar las cosas." She leaves and Marty says "Emmy's Spanish is not very good, so please speak English if it is about her." I'm grateful for the help, but I did understand this time. He said the doctor has arrived and told her to help get things ready.

Marty turns and winks where no one can see. Oh, he wants Ricardo to think I don't understand Spanish at all. Ricardo nods and apologizes. "I'm so sorry for your injuries. I'm told it was not intentional. I will be careful to use English with you."

I nod and start to speak but Marty puts his finger to my lips to keep me from causing my face to bleed more. I want to know why he told Ricardo that he would bring me here, and for what?

I remember the IV going in and not much else until I awake in Marty's bed. He is sitting beside me, fully clothed. I guess it's still daytime because the bright sunlight is streaming through the window just past the bed. Carmen is gone. I'm still numb and feel like I've been to the dentist. You know how weird you feel. Numb, but awake.

I guess Marty felt me move because he's suddenly alert and facing me. He puts his finger to his lips, leans over and turns on the radio alarm clock by the bed. He turns the music up kind of loud. "Emmy, I am so sorry you are hurt. I never dreamed anyone would snatch you. I told Ricardo that during or right after the party would be the time to take you to Mexico but clearly Marcelo thought otherwise."

With great effort on my part I ask, "So did Ricardo orchestrate this or someone else?"

He leans in and kisses me on the forehead, "Ricardo says it was not him. He says Marcelo was trying to make up for the other mistake, when he did not get you before the game. I don't know who to believe. Ricardo is in a tough spot right now. Your parents have confirmed that they will be here for the party and now you are missing and it is ultimately his fault."

I look up and the light bulb goes on, "I get it. The party is ten days from now and if he lets me go and I talk, then all kinds of shit will break loose. If he keeps me then my parents will not come. So, what do you think he's going to do?"

It takes Marty a minute, "I'm not sure. He needs to fix it if he wants a shot at your parents. I think he's going to have to confide in you. And then rescue you from Marcelo and his crew. They are working on that now. I wanted to be there at the meeting but I didn't get an invite. I tried to bully myself into it but it didn't work either. So, here I am with you. I think he wants to handle Marcelo alone, which is not a good sign for Marcelo."

"What about Carmen? Who is she? Where is she?" It's all I can think to ask.

Marty shakes his head turns down the music a little and smiles, "You are always worrying about others. Carmen is fine. She helped the doctor yesterday and then went home to her family. She looked tired. She should be back soon to sit with you while I see what is happening. You have not even asked about yourself."

I huff, "There is not much I can do about it, is there? I could use a mirror so I can look at the damage. What did the doctor say about it?"

Marty stands and heads for the bathroom and returns with a mirror. "Here is a mirror, my sweet one. Look, it's going to be okay, I think." He then turns up the music again.

I realize he did that so the listeners would have something to listen to and not think we have done anything to the connection. I do look at my face and I realize he is right. There are these funny looking bandages on me and no stitches that I can see.

Marty reaches for the music and down goes the volume, "According to the doctor, there was a small piece of gravel embedded under the skin. He removed it and stitched you internally. The little strips on the outside will fall off and there shouldn't be a scar, or at least not much of one."

I breathe a sigh of relief. "My parents will surely notice either way. The black eye that I now sport is going to be hard to hide, not to mention the cut. Did he say how long before this is healed?"

A bigger smile from Marty and I can't figure out why. "You

will see the doctor tomorrow so you can ask him then. As for your parents, we have two weeks." He reaches over and turns the music back up.

"That was good Emmy, make them worry about your parents. Let's see what the plan is. When Carmen is back and here with you, I will go see. Until then, rest. You need it. You still look like shit."

I smack him hard on the arm and I shouldn't have because that kind of effort hurt all over.

"Thank you, kind sir, for the compliment."

FORTY-SIX

Houston OPS

- Agent Carmen Galvez has reported in. Kitten had minor plastic surgery at the house in River Oaks to repair a gash to her chin. She also has a black eye.
- Agent Wells is back in the house with her.
- Agent Galvez will be back on duty with Kitten shortly.
- Kitten's parents have been notified.
- As soon as we know what the plans are there, we will put our plan together here.

FORTY-SEVEN

Double Doug Deception

THE NEXT DAY, CARMEN AND I take a walk in the garden. It is so nice to be outside even though I know we are being watched. Carmen and I walk to the very far edge of the property. The yard is large and covered with trees, but I can still see houses all around us. The houses are large like this one. I can hear lawn mowers in the distance. If I needed to, I think I can climb any one of these big oaks and drop down on the other side into someone else's yard. Which of the neighbors would help me? I can feel the beginning of a plan. Which way and tree would be best?

Just as I am about to verbalize my thoughts to Carmen, a golf ball drops in front of her and she screams and drops to the ground. Boy, can she scream! Was she hit, is she hurt? The guard starts towards us, she jumps up and yells, "No es necessario. Es solo una pelota desde el patio detras de nosotros." He stops. She picks up the ball to show him and says, "He doesn't need to come to us. It is just a ball from the yard behind us." The guard turns and heads back.

I look around and I can see a few more on the ground. As I start to collect them, I hear a voice from above. "Those are mine. Sorry, I hope I did not hurt anyone." This is a voice I've heard before. Standing on a very large limb that is spanning his yard into this one is the golfer I made the derby for, Doug... Something.

His mouth has dropped open. "Wow, what happened to you? Did you get that in the Derby chase? You look awful."

I am stunned at his straightforwardness, "Why, thank you. You look nice, too."

Even though he is high up above me, I can see him pale. "Sorry, crap. That just slipped out. But you know that black eye is something to behold."

"Thanks, Mr. Obvious. Why are you throwing golf balls at us?"

This time he blushes, "Uh, I'm not throwing them at you really. I was just practicing chip shots, and that one got away from me. Are you okay?"

My brain immediately sees the benefit of knowing that his yard could be a safe yard to escape to if needed so I probe deeper. "So, do you live here? Do I need to worry about being in this part of the yard in the future?"

At this, he sits on the limb, "My parents bought this house in River Oaks for me to use while I am here at college. It's bigger than I need, so some of the team live here, too. There are four of us. It's close to the River Oaks country club and the golf course, and not too far from campus. Do you live here?"

I look back at the house and see the guard standing close to the house but not within earshot. "No, I'm a guest while I get better. Carmen, she's a friend and a nurse, so she is making sure I'm ok. I took a nasty fall during the Derby Chase."

He looks over his shoulder and waves at someone. "Be down in a minute. Hey, gotta go. But, thank you for the derby. The girl that took it from me was very generous with her kisses since I kind of let her take it rather than end up injured in a tackle like you."

My brain is trying hard to take in where I am and what to say next. I've been to the country club for dinner with my parents and it is simply a beautiful place. River Oaks is a neighborhood with stunning estates and wealthy people.

I need to keep the conversation going but I can see Carmen cut her eyes to the house.

She steps close, "Marty and Ricardo are coming." I nod.

At this, I turn and call to Marty, "Mi amor, look who is our neighbor. It's the golfer that I decorated a derby for. He is telling me how attractive my black eye is that I got from the derby chase. He surrendered, rather than end up like me. In the future, I need to do like him so I do not get hurt."

Marty emerges from behind a small bush, smiles and waves, "Hey there, nice to meet you. I'm Caesar. Is that your home?"

This guy looks so relaxed on his perch. "Like I was telling Emmy, my dad bought it for me to use while I am here at college. Sorry about the golf balls in the yard. There are four of us here and we try to be careful. If you think about it, just throw them back over. Gotta go. Time to go to the course."

He was up and gone in a flash.

I turn back to Ricardo and Marty, and am surprised to see that Carmen has gone. "Hi, boys. What's up?"

Ricardo was the first to speak. "I'm glad to see that you feel well enough to take a walk. We have just been talking about what happened to you. Can we go back to the house, sit and talk?"

I put my hand in Marty's outstretched hand and we follow Ricardo back through the yard to the covered deck. Before we walk away, I throw the couple golf balls I have found over the fence.

There are drinks on a tray waiting for us thankfully, because I'm thirsty and tired, too. I guess surgery has that effect on you.

Ricardo seems a little nervous to me. His voice is soft and reassuring when he starts. "Emmy, I know your injury has been quite the misfortune, brought on by Marcello's mistake. I am sincerely sorry for that. He has been disciplined and it will not happen again. I hope you will forgive him. The girls thought he was under orders from me. That plan was not from me. They were so surprised he did that on his own. Your derby was turned in to the fraternity with a donation to the Sigma Chi's president. He sent you a thank you note and I have it here."

He pushes an envelope towards me. "All your sorority friends have been told that you were injured but will be just fine. I hope that this unfortunate mistake will not damage our budding friendship. Caesar is rightfully angry with Marcelo. I have taken the liberty of ordering lunch to be served out here, if that is okay?"

This man is nothing if not gracious. What can I say, I am his captive…guest, according to him. He is waiting for an answer when I look up. "I do not hold you responsible for this. I do need to get back to my place so I can study for finals. My art studio time is limited and today is one of them. I need to get busy and finish my work, not to mention study for my anatomy final."

Ricardo relaxes a little with my focus on school. "Yes, Caesar did explain that you must put in studio time and you are missing it today, so I took the liberty of calling an associate to arrange a replacement time since you were injured and had surgery. He was very accommodating and said for you to pick a time and he will make the arrangements."

Okay, wow, that was nice. I guess he doesn't want me running out of here screaming "bad men live here." I pull out my best 'talk-to-important-people smile, voice and vocabulary' to respond.

"I'm ever so grateful to you for your help. I'm sure my parents will be grateful, too. They are excited to visit in May. I'd love to tell them, when I call them, as to when and where that will be."

I can feel Marty flinch. Wonder what I've just said that was wrong. Oh well, too late now to worry.

Ricardo is interrupted by lunch arriving. After all is served, he puts his hand on mine and explains that the formal invitations were mailed yesterday and my parents should have them soon. Okay, that was quick. How did he know I would play along with this charade?

I clear my voice and touch my tender chin, "That is good to know. Then all I need to do is study. I would love to have a copy of the invitation for my scrapbook, if possible."

He nods. Eating is slow and it hurts, but I know I need to eat. After lunch, Marty and I take a slow walk to a bench under an oak tree in the back and sit to talk. I don't care where we are, but I want to go home now.

Marty starts, "I know you want to leave right this minute but trust me, it needs to be in the morning."

I do trust Marty so I frown but nod. "Okay"

FORTY-EIGHT

Houston OPS

- Kitten's apartment has been swept for foreign listening devices and cameras.
- Charlie will be across the courtyard in Sterling's apartment to keep a close eye on things.
- Agent Suzanna Williams is flying in to stay with Kitten as a best friend from home. She will shadow her during the next two weeks.
- Security for Big Bird and Whitey are coming from Washington with them. They will be staying in a home in the River Oaks area for this event.
- River Oaks Country Club is secure for the party.

FORTY-NINE

Finals

———

I'M HAPPY TO BE BACK in my apartment. The first thing I notice is the smell of Italian food as I step in the door. Marty doesn't seem to be disturbed at all. I can hear some female voice singing, "Que Sera, Sera" from the kitchen. Seconds later, I'm hugged warmly by a complete stranger. She whispers in my hair, "Hug me back. The curtains are open and I think someone is watching."

Okay, I can play this game. I hug her and whisper, "Who are you? And what are you doing in my apartment?"

Marty steps in and hugs her, too. "Suzanna, it's been a long time since we've seen you. When did you get in? You were supposed to be my surprise for Emmy."

Suzanna on cue, "I caught an earlier flight from DC and got a taxi from the airport. The nice apartment manager let me in after I showed her the invitation to the party."

Alright, another agent. I look towards the kitchen. "I'm so glad you're here and it is an amazing surprise!" I hug her again. "I didn't know you could cook! Whatever it is, smells too good to wait another minute to eat. Do you guys mind if I close the drapes? The afternoon sun makes it so hot in here." I walk over to the window and pull it closed.

Suzanne looks straight at me and delivers the next sentence naturally but I know it is rehearsed. "You're right, up until I went to college and had to learn to cook, I was awful. Things change when you need to learn to survive without a cook. Mom just laughs at me now when I follow the cook around the kitchen at home trying to learn."

Suzanna pushes a button and reacts first, "That was great on your part. I thought you knew I would be here. Why didn't you tell her? Doesn't matter now."

I look back and forth to both of them, "Can we talk freely? I mean, isn't the place bugged?"

Suzanna smiles, "Yep, bugged, but not now jammed for our convenience. Right this minute, they are checking on the signal because I pressed this little button right here and jammed them. We will turn it off and on so they won't be aware we found it. If we don't let them hear anything, they might try to put another in here."

"Okay," is all I can say. I'm hungry and tired. Suzanna has made my day with the spaghetti and meatballs she's fixed. We unjam the buds while we eat. Marty tells us he has things to do and leaves. Suzanna puts a radio next to the plant where she says the bug is and turns up the music. I don't care what she does, I'm heading to bed.

Suzanna sweetly says, "Night, Emmy. See you in the morning."

As chance will have it, or maybe not, I bump into the golfer and his buddies in the parking lot on my way to studio time with Suzanne in tow. They all stop and Doug does introductions. They have just finished a final and are on their way to the club to play golf. Doug asks, "Did you know my parents know your parents?"

All of my warning alarms go off. Anyone getting too close, too soon, scares me, especially lately.

"Oh really? I don't know you except your name and that you play golf." I can see the guys think this is humorous and I hate embarrassing him. I might need to climb that fence and have them rescue me some time. So, I continue. "Do your parents live here, too? How do they know each other?"

He smacks one of the guys who is snickering and says, "I think our parents have mutual friends in politics. Anyways, I'm sure you know while the four of us are away for the weekend at a golf tournament, your parents and mine will be at the house in River Oaks for some party."

I don't say a word, but Suzanne steps in. "Yeah, Emmy's mom

told my mom all about it. So, you're the guy in the tree. What a small world. Emmy was supposed to be surprised, but that's out of the bag now."

I can see Doug is nervous now, thinking he spoiled something. I decide to rescue him. "Doug, she's playing with you. This is Suzanne and she is my best girlfriend from high school, here for the party. She came early and you did not spoil a surprise. I was very aware my parents were coming into town. I just didn't know where they were staying. I'm sure I will meet your parents then. Look, I'm on my way for some studio time so I've gotta go…bye."

I turn to leave and Doug reaches out to stop me. "Hey I might need some help packing since I have to vacate the house for the weekend. Wanna help?"

Yikes, that's crazy. Suzanne doesn't even hesitate. "I would love that, but only if you show me your favorite tree in your back yard."

"Cool, no problem, it's a deal. He magically whips out a card with his address and phone number on it. "I'll be home after dark. Call so we can talk."

Suzanne chuckles and we walk on. I turn and see the other guys pat him on the shoulder and they get into two different parked cars.

Suzanne is smiling, "I was wondering how I was going to get into his house. Problem solved. That little puppy doesn't know what he is in for."

As we approach the Fine Arts building, I realize she is waiting for me to talk. "You know, Charlie and Sterling checked him out and he runs with a fast crowd of rich kids from the East Coast. I'm surprised my parents are friends with his parents."

She rolls her eyes, "Well, duh, I read those reports too. I didn't think I was his type. You never know, I guess, what men see and or don't see. He obviously doesn't realize I am at least four no five years older than him, then again maybe that was what the others were patting him on the shoulder about."

I scrunch my eyebrow together, "You mean he likes older women?"

"Careful missy. I'm not older by much and yes, some men

prefer older women. Some day, you may be in my shoes. Well, maybe not… You seem to get engaged a lot."

I guess what she said registered, and then she saw my face and realized she had crossed an invisible line.

"Yes, I have been engaged before and I'd like to think Charlie and I are headed that way some day. This engagement is to help with this group, but dang when you put it like that, it hurts."

Suzanne quickly apologizes, "Hey, that came out wrong. It really was meant as a compliment. I've never been asked and I guess my jealousy came out. Sorry."

I try to smile but I'm not so sure how it looked, "It's the truth and sometimes the truth is hard to swallow. I need tougher skin."

Studio time is at least productive. I finish most of the projects I need for my portfolio. I need to submit it in two days. I am sure I can get that done.

I am exhausted when we get back to the apartment. My energy level rises when I see Sterling and Charlie sitting on the sofa waiting for us. Sterling is up and has Suzanne heading for the door before she has a chance to protest. I hear Sterling say, "I need food and they need time."

I sit down next to Charlie. "I'm hungry, too. I'm hungry for you."

There's no need for more words. He swings me over his shoulder and we're behind closed doors in no time. Some time later, we hear Sterling.

"Shit, the bedroom door is still closed. We shouldn't be here yet. I promised I'd keep you busy so they could get busy. We need to leave."

Charlie sighs but goes to the bedroom door, "Too late, you two came in like a pack of elephants. Did you bring us food? If not, go right back out and get some."

Suzanne holds up a bag and cute little boxes that are undeniably Chinese takeout. Yum.

I had three things left to do. Number one was definitely alone time with Charlie and that was amazing. Number two is to check on my grade from my anatomy final. And three, get a dress for the party. I need to go by the classroom and look at the posted grades by ID number. That's not a problem. I just don't feel like shopping with my lovely black eye. On campus, I certainly get stares, but in public it is ten times worse.

Suzanne, Marty and I go out late the next morning to see what my final grade is in Anatomy. I hoped for an A or 4.0 and I got at 3.5. I guess that's close enough for a non-biology student. We decide to celebrate by going to the Mexican restaurant we met Ricardo after the Final Four.

Well, surprise surprise, as Gomer Pyle on TV says. The gang's all here. I introduce Suzanna to Ricardo's group and we join their table. It is a slow day for the restaurant, so we have the place almost to ourselves.

As we sit down with them, everyone has taken their turn to study my green and purple-black eye. The bandages are gone from my chin but the shiner is still big and green with purple edges.

Cecilia asks, "Do you have a dress for the party?"

I moan, "No, I don't want to go shopping looking like this. So many people stare. I thought I might send Suzanna out to find me something."

Cecilia is visibly shocked, "Why have you not asked me? I thought you liked what I found last time."

Oh, heavens, is she going to cry? "Uh, I thought you would be too busy studying to shop for yourself, so adding me to the task I thought would be too much to ask. Your choices for me were spot on and I would love your help. Maybe we should think of something that goes with my new eye color."

I think it's funny, but she is appalled. Suzanna laughs and says, "Emmy, if it still shows by then, makeup will cover it. I'm good at that. I have to be, I'm not as lucky as you to have perfect skin. Cecilia, I'll get the hair and makeup and you can be in charge of the rest. Maybe we can shop and have lunch on Friday?"

I think Suzanna's idea of shopping and lunch is good but Cecilia is way too excited. Marty even notices. With a few more words, we have a time and a place to shop decided on. I want to drive but that is turned down. Ricardo says he will have a car and driver for us. Cecilia frowns. I elbow Marty and he chimes in with, "I want to do it this time. It's my turn." I turn, kiss him and say thanks before anyone else can stop the plan. Cecilia is now smiling. Maybe she needs a break from her man. I'm sure, when we are alone, she will tell me.

FIFTY

Houston OPS

- Big Bird and Whitey will be at the Ballentine's River Oaks house while here in Houston.
- Surveillance is being set up on property as we speak. This property backs up to Ricardo's place and cameras are being installed in the big oak. They will appear to be lights pointed at the pool area to most eyes.
- Their son, Douglas, and his three teammates live there during the school year. Vet all the teammates.
- Everyone has an assignment for the party. Check your folders.

FIFTY-ONE

River Oaks Country Club

RIVER OAKS COUNTRY CLUB WAS built in 1923. John Staub was hired to design a two-story revival Spanish clubhouse. I got all that stuck in my head from my architectural drawing class. The club is mostly known for the tennis tournaments it's hosted since 1931. It also has a tournament-quality golf course just north of the clubhouse.

When you pull up to the front in its semi-circle driveway, you expect to see women with large hooped skirts come through the doorway. This party is going to be grand. Just thinking about this place, I realize that my dress will have to match the site in grandeur.

"Emmy, are you asleep?" Charlie is in my face and looks concerned.

I open my eyes to his beautiful ones staring down. "I'm awake. Oh, shit." I see the clock and know I'm supposed to be up and out the door in ten minutes.

Charlie is dressed and Suzanne is standing behind him. "Why didn't you two wake me up earlier?"

"I did... She did, too. You even talked to me," was Charlie's response.

I didn't even answer, I knew he was right. I bound out of bed and head to the bathroom, aiming to be ready in record time. I'm dressed and ready in 15 minutes. I have my hair in a ponytail and have slipped on a short casual dress and platform heels. No running for me today in these, but I love them. I bought them in a small boutique in New York just after Christmas and have been waiting for the right weather to wear them. They are brown sandals on three-inch platform heels. Inserted in the heel is a snow globe with tiny plastic flowers inside. When you walk, the snow and the flowers move. So fun.

Marty is in the living room when I appear and is more than ready to go. All he says is, "You're late."

He is on his way to the door and I just talk to his back. "Sorry."

In the parking lot, Suzanne is already in the back seat and frowns at me. "I'd make some snide remark but Charlie didn't even stay last night. Didn't you sleep well?"

"I don't know. I was dreaming I was awake... Has that ever happened to you?"

Both look at me like I'm nuts so I drop the subject and just sit quietly.

Suzanna leans over the back seat, "I know this has nothing to do with today's mission but I need to see those shoes you have on."

My head whips around and I get nervous, "Do you mean mine?

She is pointing and smiling, "Yes, I do mean those killer shoes." I look down and I notice Marty looking, too.

"Come on, pass one back." Suzanne is wiggling her fingers in anticipation of touching my cool shoes.

I pass a shoe back to her and she giggles like a five-year-old. She is shaking it and cooing over it as the flowers float around inside.

"These are the coolest shoes I've ever seen. Where did you get them? I think they are my size, can I borrow them sometime?" She's not even looking at me when she says that, her eyes are glued to the snow globe.

I answer he and say yes, she can borrow them. She's cooing at them like a baby again.

Marty ends this fun by speeding out of the parking lot, making us slide sideways and hold on for dear life. What's wrong with him? Being a few minutes late can't be that bad.

Suzanne hands my shoe back and starts looking over some notes and Marty says "Destroy that... Not a good thing to get into the wrong hands."

She mumbles. "Okay, but where." Then louder she states, "I'm going to quiz Cecilia about the details of the party and I don't want to forget anything. I'm sure she is a wealth of information just waiting to be sucked dry."

Marty rolls his eyes and has a wolfish grin, "There are so many comebacks to that but none are appropriate. Hand it over."

Suzanna hands over a small three by five card and he eats it. She laughs, "That's one solution. Just so you know, I could have used poison ink, but alas I didn't."

Marty sort of chokes, "Let's get on the same page. Our number one mission today is to get some idea of what the plan is for the party. Well, after the dress hunt." All agree.

Cecilia practically runs to get in the car when we pull up. She must have been waiting by the door. I can't help but feel like something is wrong. I need to talk to Marty, well Suzanna and Charlie, too, about what I'm picking up. Maybe they know something I don't. Duh, they probably do.

Many hours and dresses later, we each have one to wear. Before we drop Cecilia off, I manage a word in private to her. "Cecilia, if you ever need me, please call. I will help no matter what." Her reaction is a hug and she whispers into my ear, "You don't know how grateful to know that. Thank you." As she leans back, "Emmy I'm just as happy as can be and I will call if I need your help with my dress. It is so nice of you to offer. I will tell Ricardo of your generosity." I smile and step back to let her go, feeling even more concerned.

Back in the car Susanna places her hand on my shoulder from the back seat and leans in, "What was that all about?" I shake my head, "I really don't know. I'm so concerned for her. That statement is so telling of the pressure she is under."

"She's getting into a marriage that she doesn't want but she cannot escape from. I think she hates Ricardo. I know hate is a strong word but once you get past Ricardo's façade, he is mostly self-centered and self-important. If she has allowed him to see her true distaste for him, she should be worried."

Marty's opinion doesn't help with my worry for her it only enhances it. Suzanna nods her head, "I got the same vibe. Emmy, she seems to trust you. Hold that close. It may come to serve you well."

"Yikes, I will keep both of your ideas in my head and be careful. She is going to look stunning in that red flamenco style dress. It fits her like a glove and it will turn every man's head at the party. I hope Ricardo can handle that kind of attention."

Marty clears his throat, "I think Ricardo wants her for that. She makes him look good. He is not interested in her as a person. He wants a plaything, something to dangle on his arm. Remember this is a business marriage, not a love marriage."

In my head I know that but hearing it out loud makes me shiver. I'm so glad I don't have that problem. "Do you think she will betray him if given a safe way out, or will she be loyal to her family? I mean, it took two families to make this arrangement."

Suzanna answered, "She's a wild card. There's no way to know for sure. I think, if she feels she can escape and not get hurt or killed, she would bail. But that's just my gut feeling. She's revealed nothing for sure to me. She came closest to confirming she wanted out with you just now."

That statement gives me much to think about and I'm silent all the way home. By the time we arrive home and get our dresses hanging up so they don't wrinkle, I'm in no mood to try anything on and I just want some time to myself with Charlie. Charlie suggests a trip to the pool and I agree. It's late in the afternoon but still Houston hot. The pool water is warm from the sun but Charlie is hot. I don't mean his skin is hot, but that he looks hot in his cutoffs he's using as a swimsuit. After a long day with Marty who's on edge, and Suzanna who's all business, except for that out-of-character moment with my shoe, I'm ready for this time with Charlie.

"Kitten... Emmy, I miss you. I hate it when Marty gets to spend all day with you. It makes me a little jealous. I hate it that you're involved again. I will be glad when I don't have to share you. I've made plans for us to travel back to your home in D.C. We leave two days after the party. I can't wait."

Charlie hasn't called me Kitten in months. It makes me think that I'm more a job and not just a regular girlfriend. I long for that time and he is right, the three-day drive home will be something both of us need. "Charlie, I'm so ready to spend day after day with just you. I'm so sorry that I can't be just a regular girlfriend. Someone you can disappear from your job with and just have fun. That day will come."

Charlie's face blanches, "I never want you to think of yourself as my job. I could have opted out of this detail. I want to be near you. Let's swim. You need the exercise and so do I," he says with a wink.

With that, we spend maybe an hour just trying to just exist as normal people. Charlie has gotten out of the pool and I'm swimming toward the steps when Marty jumps into the pool with a big splash right next to me. As he surfaces, he pulls me close and holds on tight. He spins me around and talks up against my ear, "Ricardo and his goons are steps behind me. He has found out that you live here and not the fake apartment. Play it cool. I've got this."

I look up to see Ricardo with a full entourage of beefy men just opening the gate. Suzanne has appeared out of nowhere and is sitting in Charlie's lap. Marty is planting a drippy kiss on me and I am back in the scary game.

"Mi amor, you are so sexy in this suit. You make me crazy," Marty says loudly. He whispers, "Act little put-off. You have a new place because you felt too caged up at my place. You still love me, just need space to study and have some privacy." He picks me up and holds me in the air and then slowly lowers me into a kiss. "Come say hi to the boys. I want you to meet some of Cecelia's cousins just in from Mexico."

As I climb out of the pool, Suzanna hands both of us a towel and I can see Charlie is gone. When I turn back to Marty, Ricardo is just a few feet away. His intense smile scares me to death. I return the smile and wrap the towel around myself. I am wearing a very skimpy bikini and there are five, six counting Marty, pairs of eyes checking me out. It is, to say the least, quite uncomfortable.

"Hi, Ricardo. I see you've found my hideout. I'm staying with Suzanna for the last few weeks before I go home. Who are your friends?" Suzanna steps up and does a cute little wave and all but Ricardo smile. She's also wearing a tiny bikini and these men are openly enjoying the view and she knows it. I think she is attempting to put their minds somewhere else and it's working. Go, girl.

Ricardo, the ever-present businessman, introduces the group of men. I won't remember all their names but I'm sure Suzanna will. All bear some resemblance to Cecilia, so I'm sure they are closely related. Marty saved the day, "We stopped by to take you two to dinner."

Suzanna comes to the rescue. "Oh, this is hard to refuse. Emmy and I are meeting her parents for a late dinner. They arrive sometime around nine and we will meet them at the home in River Oaks where they are staying. The party is in a day and a half, we have so much to do. Please forgive us, and know I would love to spend more time with all of this muscle."

Ricardo has a schooled face but I can see the slight hint of anger before he manages a gracious smile, "Cecilia will be disappointed, but I'm sure she will understand. Say hello to your parents for me and I look forward to meeting them at the party."

Marty has toweled off and is almost dry. He pulls on his shirt and shoes and turns, "I need a kiss, mi amor, before I leave, and a private word."

Marty scoops me up and walks over to the table across from the gate, puts me down and kisses me. While I am wrapped in his arms he says, "Tell Suzanna I think two of these men are assassins, here to take out your mom and dad. She will know what to do. I saw Charlie on the balcony taking photos so make sure he gets good intel. Be on alert and keep safe, go nowhere alone and I mean nowhere."

With that, he takes my hand and walks back to the waiting group. One more sweet kiss and they are gone. Suzanna sort of sighs, "Whew, that was close. Thank God, Marty gave us a two-minute heads up or you would have been in Charlie's arms. Charlie saw my warning signal and jumped out of the pool. Good thing you are slow."

At this point, I don't care how that happened, I'm just grateful. "Are my mom and dad really arriving tonight?"

As always, Suzanna's answer has me tilting my head, "Yes and no. They are on the ground now at Ellington Air Base but they will make an entrance later for the bad guys' sake. We will wait for them at the Ballentine home. You remember, where the golfer was in the tree."

I can't wait to hug my parents and ask them why in hell's name are they here putting themselves at risk. As soon as that thought ran through my mind, I knew the answer. I can practically hear dad say, 'it's our job, not yours. We signed up for this.' I have smart parents and, most of all, brave.

Charlie, Marty, and Suzanna are with me, plus a lot of others, at this beautiful home. It's hard to believe four college boys live here. It has eight bedrooms and guest quarters by the pool that can accommodate two more. There might be staff quarters, too, but I haven't explored the place yet. Doug and his teammates were someplace in Arizona for a tournament. I was assigned his room for the weekend. It is neat as a pin.

Mom and dad arrive right on time with a procession deserving of dad's new job title, Secretary of Labor, Veterans Affairs. The vehicles come through the gate at record speed. The gate closes off any prying eyes and I understand why they hurried when the doors open. So many people get out of the cars and limo, it's like watching one of those old clown cartoons where fifty people exit a Volkswagen. Mom and dad are part of the mass of people and I run in for my much-needed hugs.

There's no standing around and we are ushered inside quickly. The smiles on their faces deceive what is hiding inside, I know. I have seen this fake smile many times in my life. Never show on the outside what is going on inside, except maybe to trusted friends or family. The team inside is trusted, but his concern is personal.

Mom, Dad, and I go toward the small study just off the entrance, and Charlie, Marty, and Sean start to follow. Dad stops, "Boys, I need a moment with my girls." That was all it took for the three to stop dead, turn and head away from the door. When the door closes, mom is up in my face, looking at my eye, which is now just a little yellow, and my chin. "Are you okay? This looks so much better than the pictures I saw."

Dad sits on the chair by the desk and mom leads me to the little loveseat. Both of us look at dad, waiting for him to start.

"Before either of you hear any of the plans, I want you to know that if at any time it is too much or there is something wrong at this party, act sick and we'll leave. No questions asked. We will just excuse ourselves and go. Do both of you understand?"

Mom and I nod, although I'm sure they've talked about this earlier on and this is for my sake.

"Dad, getting these guys might help with more than one problem, right? I mean, not just the Rat Line, but drugs and trafficking of people. Ricardo and his crew are into everything. They're scary."

Mom puts her arm around my shoulder, "That's why we have a back-up plan. There are some times when you get enough intel that it is necessary to change tactics. We are not here to have a physical fight, just to pull you out safely and have enough info to put an end to this group."

I can see they are waiting for me to speak. "I understand the danger and I'm not sure how this could end without someone getting hurt, but I'm here to follow orders and help. Marty is in deep and I worry about him."

Dad's lips thin and I know he's worried, too. "Emmy, Marty has trained for this opportunity all his career and he's as ready as he can be. He's not going to take you down this path with him. He thinks you've been amazing during this time and that he couldn't have gotten this far without you. Tonight is just a way to push him deeper in by making him the bad guy who is certainly not suitable for our lovely daughter."

With the pep talk over, dad steps over to the door, opens it, and a huge group steps in. "Let's get the main info out and then break into teams." Several 'yes sirs' comes from the crowd.

I have three teams to meet with, plus Marty. The first one is the easiest, I think. It's with two women and my dress. It appears my dress is wired and traceable. I even have a necklace that's a tracker.

"Gosh, so if my clothes get taken, I still have this." Both look up, surprised. The older lady says, "Let's hope that doesn't happen. Keep your clothes on."

Crap, I was trying to be funny but these two are all business. The younger woman finishes making sure nothing is showing,

"Don't mind Betty, she's the best at this stuff. All of the additions to your dress are small compared to what has been added to the country club. This will help if you get separated from Marty." I have no intentions of leaving Marty's side. Well, unless I'm with my parents. "Yes, ma'am. I will be careful."

Next, is a tour of the back yard. Sean is standing next to me with a note that says, "look, but don't talk," on it. Then we go inside to see what surveillance equipment is set up out there. There are cameras watching not only this yard, but Ricardo's, too. Sean introduces me to a three-man team of hunky soldiers.

"These men will be on duty in the trees in the back of this yard, overlooking Ricardo's home. If, for some reason, you or anyone goes back there during or after the party, they will extract anyone who comes to the back area and says, 'look at the beautiful stars.' Understand that this is an emergency extraction team. They will grab you and pull you up and out."

I look from one to the other, nod and smile. They don't smile back. They are military-still. I thank them and go on to my next team.

Team three is about food. Sean stands by and listens. A charming short man explains that he is the cook at the club and will be watching what goes out. My parents and I are not seated together, so there will be several servers who are assigned to us.

"Why is this necessary? I mean, they're not going to poison me, are they?" He smiles, "Non, mademoiselle. But maybe try to put you to sleep with a drug. There are several that are slow-acting but very effective. If your waiter calls you 'mademoiselle' then you will know he or she is one of us and it is okay to eat. D'accord?"

My knowledge of French is ok, and so I agree back in French. "Oui monsieur, je suis d'accord." I'm beginning to hate this party. I need to reel back my emotions... Tonight, I need to be in the present, not lost in emotions.

All three meetings are done, now for my check-in with Marty. He's with a bunch of men in the downstairs formal dining room. When he sees me, he steps away and comes close.

"Are you okay? You look stressed. Come with me."

We walk down the hall, heading outside. Once on the patio,

we sit facing each other knee to knee. "I know I cannot say a thing that will change tonight and help you. There are a lot of people here to fix this and shut this little group down. I will get caught up in the takedown and you shouldn't worry about me. I think back to that day at the Hilton, when I kissed you for the first time." Marty's breathing is ragged and he takes a deep breath.

"I wonder what would have happened if you had chosen me and not Charlie? I'm not sure if I would feel any better today knowing how dangerous Ricardo is, that you are walking willingly into this nest with me. I want you to know, and I have told Charlie as well, that I will do my best to get this right tonight. I'm not even sure what right is, but you are my priority. Tonight, if you call me Caesar, I will begin our evacuation protocol."

Marty has become more than a friend. He feels like a brother… Well, that's not right either because you can't kiss a brother the way we have. He's simply the best. I smile, reach out and put my hand on the side of his jaw. He leans into my hand and for the first time, I feel him tremble. He realizes his mistake and leans back. He let me see too much of his fear and worry. My superhero is human.

"Marty, I'll be okay. You're the best and we need these guys gone, or at least on the way to being locked up." He takes my hands and says, "I should say you're the bravest girl I know, but you aren't the girl I met nine months ago. You're an amazing woman. If you ever want to kick Charlie to the curb, even though he is my best friend, you call on me, deal?"

"Okay Marty, it's a deal." With that small moment over, we head back in.

I have one last thing I would like to do, and that is to find Charlie.

He's coming out to the patio as we're heading in. "Hey man, can I have a moment with my girl? You'll have her all evening."

Marty doesn't even speak, he just pats Charlie on the shoulder and is gone. Charlie has been seen around me too much in public and he might be spotted as surveillance at the country club. Charlie takes my hand and walks me to my room and at the door, I sneak a kiss. I'm sure in this house, someone is watching. He enters, closes the door and leans over the desk and writes me a note. When I look puzzled, he points, so I pick it up to read. It says, "I will be here in the trees watching. I can see the back of Ricardo's house. If you need me immediately and cannot get to the back trees, lift your dress like you're trying to step over a puddle. I will be on my way immediately with help."

He crumbles up the note, puts it in his pocket, kisses me and disappears. I take a deep breath and focus on the night ahead. Twenty minutes later, I'm ready to get my hair and makeup knocked out. To my surprise, or should I say not surprise, the two women from earlier are waiting, ready to help. Betty, the older one, watches as Aubrey applies makeup expertly and styles my hair into long, soft ringlets that cascade down my shoulders. When I look in the mirror, I wished I had watched her better because her skills are nothing short of a miracle. The yellow around my eye is gone and my skin is flawless. The makeup makes it flawless. My dress is a Halston original. The lovely blue knit is fastened at the neck and gathered at the waist in the front, leaving my back bare. There's a waistband that allows the gathered skirt to fall perfectly over my hips to the floor. My shoes match the dress and the tracker necklace looks like a real sapphire, but I know its hidden qualities. I'm so ready to get this night over with.

There's a knock on the door and I'm greeted with an amazing mom in an equally amazing outfit. She's sporting a fuchsia dress that has a full skirt like the fifties with a slit in the front with pencil slacks peering out. The slacks are some wildflower print of fuchsia, yellow, blue, and tropical green. It is the latest fashion, hot of the runway in New York for this spring and she looks good in it. "Mom, that is stunning! No one could lose you in a crowd. I love it."

Mom laughs out loud. "That's the purpose of this getup, to make me visible. And if the skirt gets in the way, I can rip it off."

Shock must have been written all over my face. "I never thought about that." The seriousness of this night is really sinking in. I will be glad when it's over and I can go home.

"Emmy, do you really need to drive your car home? We can

rent one for you at home and garage this one here and then you could fly back home and have your car here without the aggravation of a long drive." Okay, my mom's old fashioned and probably hasn't considered why I want to drive it home after school is out. I'm not sure if I should share the fact that I want to have alone time with Charlie.

"Mom, I'll think about it. Tonight is where my head needs to be now, ok?" She nods, grabs my hand and we head downstairs. Marty will meet us at the country club, so mom, dad and I climb into the waiting limo. To my surprise, Sean and Mike are in the limo dressed in bodyguard suits and armed, I'm sure. I had never thought about how mom and dad always go places with someone watching their backs. Welcome to the real world of espionage.

Within five minutes, we have made it to the circle drive of the country club and are third in line. Mom and dad are checking last-minute timelines for tonight. According to the conversation mom had with the party planner, she said there is a formal introduction of the couples' parents, then a champagne toast at six, followed by the seating of the guests for dinner, then dancing.

"How long are we staying after the dancing begins?" Dad asks. He's all about sticking to the schedule.

Mom starts in with her idea of the night. "I think Emmy should dance with her dad first and Marty should dance with his mom, then we can switch back. Add five or six more dances and the we can excuse ourselves. Your excuse, Emmy, is that you want to spend time with us and Marty with his parents. Besides, the other guests are her family and his, so we'll be out of place. I'll make sure we talk to everyone before, during, and after dinner. Sean, can you make sure we don't miss anyone?"

Sean nods. "I will be at Whitey's seven and Mike will be with you. Everyone else is keeping Emmy in sight and Marty has orders not to leave her side."

I'm just in awe of this well-oiled team. You can see they have done this before. Dad sees we are the next vehicle to unload. "Okay, everyone... Showtime. Marty is right there waiting for you, Emmy."

The limo doors open, and Sean and Mike are standing next to the valet helping Mom and I out. Marty is by my side and has me by the elbow, leading me into the foyer of the country club.

"You look amazing, my love. This dress is your style and it is stunning. Did Cecilia pick it out for you?"

I turn and smile, "Thank you, I'm glad you like the dress and yes she did. Have you seen hers? It is a beautiful throwback to her Spanish heritage. I think, when she makes her entrance, you will agree she is really letting the powers that be see that she identifies with her mom's Spanish side of the family and not the Mexican side. Like I said before, something is up with her."

Marty pulls me in tight and talks into my hair. "Everyone is sure she is looking for a way out of this but doesn't know how. I can't get too close because Ricardo is a jealous and insecure man. It would be read as flirting, so see if she will talk to you tonight."

I smile and kiss him on the cheek. "I will do my best to please you. Look, here she is."

Cecilia is being helped out by a man who appears to be her dad. There are two bodyguards, standing at both sides of the car doors. Everyone stops to watch. She is a showstopper.

Cecilia has a red, strapless dress that fits her like a glove all the way past her hips, where the enormous three layers of ruffles start. It reminds me of the flamenco dresses I saw in Spain. On her, it is the perfect shade of blood red. The small crystal beads sewn down the front make it dazzle in the light. I think this designer dress must be straight off the Paris runway. I can hear Marty take a deep breath. I lean into him, "See, I told you. Be careful, if you breathe like that where Ricardo can hear you, you won't have to be close to make him jealous."

Marty's head jerks around to look at me. "Yes, I heard a hitch in your breath when you saw her. How long have you wanted her?"

Marty's cheeks actually colored and I knew I was right. "Look, Marty, I have your back. If she can be rescued, I'm here to help. Be careful tonight. Don't let anyone else see what I saw just now."

Marty stepped forward and introduced himself to Cecilia's

parents and offered his other elbow to Cecilia. "Now I have the two most beautiful young women in the state of Texas on my arms and I need to deliver Cecelia to her man."

My mom and dad are at the door with who I think must be Marty's parents. Marty stops and makes introductions to Cecilia. I'm right, tonight these two agents are his parents. Cecilia is most gracious and plays her part well, especially when Ricardo appears from nowhere. Her smile brightens and she extends her hand for him to take and he does.

Many more introductions later, four sets of parents plus Marty, Ricardo, Cecilia and I are in a lovely holding room waiting for formal introductions and this shindig to begin. I know Sean and Mike are at the door waiting with several other bodyguards. This is the farthest they will be from Mom and Dad. I think they are put just a little at ease knowing that Marty and his agents-slash-parents are in here and armed, just in case.

Ricardo, definitely in charge, opens the door at six on the dot. He turns back to us. "Okay everyone, here's how it will go. Marty, your parents are first, then Emmy's parents, then mine and last, Cecilia's. After that, Emmy and Marty, and then Cecilia and myself. So, let's get this party started."

Marty slaps him on the shoulder. "I'm with you, Ricardo. I could use that champagne, too."

Within thirty minutes, we were all introduced and seated for dinner. This party could have put any fancy wedding reception to shame. I've been to my share of flashy affairs in Washington, D.C., but this one really has the makings of a gaudy Hollywood soirée.

Marty is seated next to me, with Mom and dad on his right side and his parents to my left. The same setup for Ricardo and Cecilia, her parents next to Ricardo and his next to her. The professional photographer comes up close to the table and addresses me, "Mademoiselle, can you smile for me?" I remember being told to that if someone call me mademoiselle, they were part of the security team, so I nodded and so did Marty. "Oui, je suis d'accord," I agree in French. Oh boy, am I glad some of that high school French stayed with me.

I started to notice several other service people either speak to mom or dad, even Marty, in French. It's nice to know who the good guys are. I ate dinner, but I couldn't tell you what it was. Then, it was time to dance. Dad was up and at my side, asking me to dance and Marty had his mom by the hand, leading her with us to the dance floor. Mom and Marty's dad behind them. I found the other couple and parents were making their way to the floor as well.

As dad took me in his arms, the big band song "Fly Me to the Moon" that Frank Sinatra made famous began and we glided across the floor. Dad can dance, so this was fun. "I can't wait to do this for real at your wedding, but this charade makes me nervous, so please excuse me if I seem off. Your mother tells me I'm doing just fine. I have nerves of steel, but putting you in the crosshairs again is driving me crazy."

I hold him tighter, "It's okay, Dad. We'll get through this. I'm sure this is in good hands. Yours, specifically." He kisses me on my cheek, passes me off to the waiting Marty and retrieves mom from Marty's dad. "Mi amor, things seem to be okay. Am I missing something? I was expecting some mischief here."

Marty swings me around and the next dance begins. "I think the party is going to be quiet but Ricardo wants us to walk into his lion's den for a nightcap after the party. All the parents and the four of us."

I look up in surprise. "I don't want to go there. What did mom and dad say?"

Marty leans into my sapphire necklace and says "I'm talking to you so that this pretty blue stone, and Sean and Mike, will hear, too. I need you to take your mom to the ladies' room and tell her. I will fill your dad in. Someone else will make that decision, not you or me."

We finish the song with a twirl and I make my way to the restroom with mom. After we talk, I get mom back to dad and Marty takes my hand and leads to the dance floor. "Need to talk to my pretty blue stone again?" Marty nods and on to the dance floor we go.

"Emmy, here's what you and that pretty stone need to know. Whitey and Big Bird started working hints into conversations about spending time with you and leaving. Cecilia's dad said that they have a gift for each family back at Ricardo's house. Your dad feels like it is necessary to go to keep suspicion at bay, so we will go there with a full entourage You, me, my parents, your parents, and bodyguards. Your mother will feign sickness about twenty minutes in and we will leave. Emmy, don't drink or eat anything there. I'm sure the blue necklace will set plan B into motion. If not, Sean will tell you. He just can't get that close to me."

I smile and nod, hoping I don't look as nervous as I feel. "Emmy, if you need help, just talk to yourself. It will work." I smile and nod again.

The dance is over and we head back to the table. I can see that this party is winding down. It's close to 10 p.m. and I'm surprised to find dad talking to Cecilia's mom. They're deep in conversation, but when I get close they stop abruptly. "Sorry for interrupting, dad. I understand we are leaving?"

Dad turns and puts on his business smile. It sets me on edge whenever he does that. "No worries, we were just discussing the future wedding plans. I was telling her that although Mexico is a lovely place to get married, we have already arranged your wedding for the Cathedral of St. Matthew the Apostle in Washington, D.C. this July."

"Really, dad? That is such good news! I've always wanted to get married there. It's my fairy tale wedding dream." I gush, picking up what dad needs me to do.

Dad smiles that smile again. "Cecilia's mom says that Cecilia would like to get married in Spain, in Segovia at the castle there. Her dad wants to have it at the Cathedral of the Assumption of Our Lady in Guadalajara. He thinks that it's a mix of both worlds, since it was built in the Spanish Renaissance style with neo gothic bell towers on each side of the entrance. It was completed in the late 1600's. The towers were rebuilt after an earthquake."

I look directly at Mrs. Quintero with my response. "I'm sure the cathedral in Guadalajara is magnificent, but I have been to the castle in Segovia and I think I'd vote for the castle. It's so romantic. I'm a true admirer of the film Romeo and Juliet, which was filmed there, you know. I can understand her desire."

She's so sweet as she answers, "You don't have to sell me on the idea. My family is from there. Your Caesar is from there too, no?"

I nod. "Yes, he is. His family is from Salamanca, but some are from Italy. I think he would love a Segovia wedding, but for us it needs to be here in the U.S. Maybe we could honeymoon there."

Mom, Marty and Marty's parents come over to us. Sean approaches mom and touches her elbow. "The limo is ready to depart, are you ready?" She turns and nods. "Yes, give us two minutes."

Ten minutes later, we're all unloading at Ricardo's home. This is scary to me. I know my group is on alert. We're greeted by staff and two rough-looking young men who Ricardo angrily dismisses when he sees that all of us are wary of them. As you walk through the foyer into a seating area, you can see a large, enclosed patio and beyond that a lovely garden with pool. I'm looking to see if I can see the men watching from our side. I can't, but I'm sure Charlie is somewhere close. Mom goes straight to the enclosed patio and everyone follows. I'm so glad she does this. The closer I am to Charlie, and an escape route, the better.

Mom starts the conversation by beckoning dad closer. "Honey, this is a lovely patio, pool and garden area. I want you to remember this so I can show the designer at home what I like. I wish I had brought a camera."

Cecilia sits next to Mom, reaches into her purse and brings out the cutest camera I have ever seen. She hands it to Mom. "I meant to take pictures today, but the professional photographers were everywhere. I only took one, so there are twenty-three more left. I'm sure Ricardo wouldn't mind you taking some photos of his place. It's his pride and joy, and he loves sharing it. This little camera is a simpler version of the 35mm ones, it's called a Triad Fotron. I just love it."

My mom knows a gift horse when she sees one and hugs Cecilia. "You are so sweet to let me take a bunch now. I will start with the patio and garden then, if there are some left, I will take some candid shots of our little group. I can take the film with me have it developed and send you copies here. Is that okay?" Cecilia nods enthusiastically.

Cecelia and mom head out to the garden, chatting and taking photos. Cecelia's mom follows. I figure it's a girl thing, so I take Marty's mom by the hand and we follow. I'm not sure where Ricardo's mom went. This left all the men sittings in the enclosed patio, except Mike. He stepped outside to keep Mom and I within sight.

Marty's mom and I step close to mom and the others. "Mom see those large oak trees way back there? They're the ones in the yard where you're staying. Don't you think that is cool?"

"Emmy, interesting... yes. Cool... Well, maybe." Mom is taking lots of pictures. I can tell Ricardo's security cameras are included, as well as the windows in the back of the house. I'm sure when we get inside, she will have some important background in her photos.

Mom excuses herself to the powder room and Cecilia's parents present all of us with airline vouchers to use when we come to Ricardo and Cecilia's wedding. There are also boxes that include luggage to make the trip with. Mom and Dad act like this is a normal occurrence and accept it with grace. Sean and Mike move the boxes to the foyer. I just sit and take it in. I don't want to even think about going to Mexico anywhere near Ricardo.

Cecilia asks me to go with her back outside, she thinks she has lost her earring. The men want to help. "You all look in here. We will just check out there and be right back." I don't wait for an answer. I turn and leave with Cecilia on my heels.

"What does it look like?" I lean in, as though to inspect the other. Cecilia speaks low and slow, "I need to escape. Take me with you." I know Sean and Mike can hear this conversation. Mike had followed me out onto the patio, so he moved closer when he heard her words.

I turned my back to the house and appeared to be looking down searching, "I will help you, but not this minute. After dark, come out to the fence line where the oaks are and be dressed differently. Wear dark clothes, pants and sneakers. I will be here to take you away."

Mike bent down like there was something interesting on the

ground and said to the ground but just loud enough to hear. "We can take you from here and keep you safe, just do as Emmy says. There are friendly eyes watching you at this moment."

There is a hitch in her breath and I'm worried whether she can pull this off. Can she keep her cool? My worries disappear when she looks up and grins. "I knew you could and would help me. My parents will be okay because dad is too important for Ricardo to risk harming him. My dad will be embarrassed because of my desertion, but he can save face with my sister. My little sister is a better match for Ricardo and she is over the moon, enamored with him. She is like him, ruthless."

Cecilia turns, reaches into the top of her dress and produces the other earring. She looks at the ground and squeals, "There it is!" She points to the ground and Mike appears to pick something up and hand it to Cecelia. Only, I can see she already had it in her hand. We rush back inside with the news that it is found. Cecelia takes the other one off and hands both to her mom. "You keep these. You are much better at holding onto things than me."

I turn back to Mom. She doesn't look so good and she's holding her stomach. I go sit with her and Mike instructs the maid to alert the driver that she needs to go home.

Dad begins the goodbyes and mom hands Cecilia her camera back. "I have the film. Thank you. I wish I felt better. I will get copies of the photos back to you soon. Emmy, can you help me to the car?

I put my arm around her, "Sure, mom. Let's get you back to the house."

Ricardo is not happy. I can see this is not what he planned. Dad, ever the fixer, steps up to put people at ease. "Ricardo, it would be our pleasure if you, Cecilia, and your families would join us for dinner tomorrow night. I will send Sean back with the arrangements. I can't wait to spend time with you again. We will have the pleasure of having some other important people eating with us. The governor and his wife will be with us, too. Until then, goodbye."

Mom, Marty's parents, and I are already at the limo, and Dad has Sean and Mike at his side. Ricardo knows his plans have unraveled and that he will have to prepare for another time… I'm just hoping that won't happen at all.

Marty leans in and says, "I'm right behind you." He strode off to his car calling over his shoulder, "Ricardo, I will be back soon." I expected there to be an objection from Ricardo, but he just stood stone still… Fuming.

FIFTY-TWO

Houston OPS

- I need to know when our assets are back on friendly turf.
- The extraction of Cecilia is our first concern for the moment.
- Marty believes she has seen and learned a great deal that can help us take this group down and push the Quintero's back into Mexico for a while.
- I want the photos Big Bird took ASAP.
- Emmy and Charlie are still set to leave Texas in two days.
- Marty is our wild card now... If we can extract Cecilia safely, we are looking at the possibility of using him as a cover for her escape.

FIFTY-THREE

Cecilia

———

THE SHORT RIDE AROUND THE long block and back into the compound has everyone talking. Mike has the biggest news, even though Sean had heard it all through the blue sapphire necklace when Cecilia was asking me for help. Mom, dad and the two agents that posed as Marty's parents are thrilled with the news.

I start to add to the conversation, but Dad cuts me off with, "Let's table this until we get inside so everyone hears at once."

Thankfully the limo shoots inside the gate, they close and everyone is out of the vehicle so fast that I find myself alone for just a second. When Marty sticks his head and hand in to help me out, Charlie's voice floats through the air from behind him. Marty moves just enough to see Charlie standing behind him, smiling.

"I got this Marty. Thanks for taking care of my girl. Let's get inside to see what all the fuss is about."

Marty's eyebrows scrunch up, "Fuss? I thought everything over there went okay."

Charlie shrugs, "I haven't a clue. I was asked to report to the main dining room for a conference immediately. So, let's get there."

I'm pretty sure I know what's up, but I want to hear it firsthand from the team. All I say is, "I'm pretty sure it's about Cecilia." Charlie and Marty hustle faster and I'm struggling to keep up.

Inside, there's so much commotion in the dining room. The group stops and claps as I walk in. Oh boy, what's going on?

"Uhh... Am I missing something?"

Dad walks over and pulls me into him, "that's my girl. She doesn't even know how much she helped with Cecilia. Let's get this plan on the road! We only have a couple of hours before dark."

Marty and Charlie both turn to me and fire off their questions at once. "Is Cecilia okay?" comes from Marty. "What did you do with Cecilia?" comes from Charlie.

I don't get to answer because the meeting is called to order and Mike begins detailing out the plan.

"We're going to break into groups. The SWAT team in the trees will be joined with a couple of others for the safe extraction of Cecilia tonight at dusk. There will be a distraction team on the front side of Ricardo's house to keep everyone busy on that side of the building. Marty, you and Sterling plus an escape team will get you and Cecilia out of here safely and into hiding. Sean, you need to arrive with the arrangements for tomorrow's dinner just ahead of the distraction. We believe Ricardo will behave with you there watching. Please, break into your teams. Extraction team to the kitchen, dinner group with Sean, and Big Bird and Whitey to the living room. Last but not least, escape team to the den. Marty, Sterling should be here with a bag packed from your place any minute. You and Emmy need to go change and get into dark clothes. "

Marty looked shocked when he heard he was on the escape team. With orders given, all three of us said in unison, "Yes sir, be right back."

Charlie and I grab Marty and make him move up the stairs to change. Afterwards, Marty heads for the den, appearing okay, for now. Charlie goes with me to the extraction team meeting. I can't imagine why I am on the extraction team, but I'm here to help. My question is answered when one of the guys asks, "Are you afraid of heights? We want Cecilia to see you and know she's safe. You will have to be in the trees above her."

I'm not afraid to climb a tree and they show me the harness that I will have on so I won't fall. I'm okay with these plan. Besides, Charlie will be there, too. We will climb in thirty minutes, so we're up and moving long before the sun sets.

Marty comes out of the den and hugs me. "I don't know how you did this, but thank you."

Everyone keeps thanking me and I just haven't figured out why this is so significant. I sit down with Charlie on the steps, "I'm missing something. Talk to me." He leans in. "Cecilia wanting out means we can run the ruse that she ran away with Caesar to Spain, leaving you behind as the jilted fiancé. It let's you loose from the marriage and saves Cecilia."

I take a deep breath, "Ah, I get it. I'm so happy for Marty, too."

Charlie says, "Yeah, he won't need to be inserted into the gang and have to go to Mexico in deep cover. That was a troubling assignment."

I am taken aback, "I mean, yes, that is a nice benefit, too. But he also gets to help the girl he's fallen for."

Charlie can't control his surprise, "What? Marty and Cecilia? Are you sure?" I tilt my head and smile. "Yes, I'm sure. Ask him. Maybe you should tell Sterling. If you missed it, so did Sterling."

I hear Dad calling me to the living room. Charlie and I start towards him. "Hi, Dad and everyone. What's the plan about dinner tomorrow with Ricardo and his group?"

Dad waves both of us in. "Sean is ready to leave with the dinner arrangements so that he will arrive seconds after the distraction begins across the street from Ricardo's front gate. That will happen just as Cecilia comes to the backyard. Marty, Cecilia, and the escape team will be out of the gate and gone before Sean is finished talking with Ricardo. Cecilia's parents think she is staying with Ricardo, and Ricardo thinks she is going to be with her parents and come with them to the dinner tomorrow. Marty left and came with you, Emmy, so he is here as far as Ricardo knows. Is that clear to everyone?"

Sean appears at the door with two college-age kids. They turn out to be cadets from the Houston police academy.

"These guys are delivering fireworks to the family that lives across the street from Ricardo, which will be the diversion. One of the teens, another cadet at the house, will set off fireworks accidentally that go into Ricardo's front lawn. Is everyone ready? Charlie and Emmy, you should be in the trees by now.

Go." Sean looks like he is going to injure Charlie and me if we don't run, so we do.

Harness on and sitting on a huge branch of this old oak tree, I strain to see if Cecilia is coming. Charlie is sitting right behind me and has night goggles on. "There she is. I almost missed her. She has her blonde hair hidden in a black hoodie." Coms are on, so everyone is listening and ready to snatch her.

Cecilia has to be close enough for one of the extraction team to drop and scoop her up and then be pulled to safety. I'm excited to see how this works. Cecilia sees me as she gets closer. I smile and give the two thumbs up. In my com, I hear the word "go" and a heartbeat later there is an explosion coming from in front of Ricardo's place.

Cecilia turns to look, guards that had been trailing her turn and head back to the house. In what seems like a split second, a dark shadow drops from the tree, puts both arms around Cecilia and they are pulled up. Cecilia didn't make a sound. We all quickly leave the trees and make for the house.

Cecilia is standing stock when I approach her. "Are you okay? Welcome to your new life."

On the other side of the house, the fireworks have every one of Ricardo's men out the front door and ready for an invasion.

Cecilia hugs me and we are hustled into the house. The men who rescued her disappear before Cecilia had sense enough to thank them. "Come on, Cecilia, we need to keep you moving. You're so brave."

We are in the house and out the front in less than a minute. A big black Suburban has its doors open and Charlie beckons Cecilia to the passenger door behind the driver. Cecilia and I scurry over. Marty is sitting inside and reaches out to help Cecilia in. Cecilia gasps, "What are you doing here? Ricardo will kill you, Caesar."

Marty's smile is so sweet. "Cecilia, my real name is Marty Wells and I'm not Caesar. I will explain everything on the way. We must take a flight out of here. Goodbye, Emmy. Take care of Charlie." With that, Sterling climbs in the Suburban, doors shut and the gate opens. They're gone.

As that Suburban clears the drive, Sean's Suburban arrives

back from his mission. We all hustle back inside to the living room for a briefing from Sean. He began and all are silent.

"I pulled into the drive to give Ricardo the invitation amidst the fireworks diversion. I explained to him that one had been sent to Cecilia and her parents at their hotel. He seemed a little alarmed at first, but I told him that 'Caesar' was delivering it to Cecilia and her parents in person. The police and the firetruck arrived just as I was ready to depart. This caused a lot more chaos. They wanted IDs and were there because of the illegal discharging of fireworks inside the city limits of Houston. All the bystanders were checked and many of the witnesses were pointing fingers at the teens across the street. It was hilarious. Ricardo was so angry, but one of his goons whispered in his ear some news that caused him to storm back into the house shouting "encuentrala" which, I bet, means "find her." I wish I could have stayed to see the chaos inside."

The whole living room was cheering. Dad raised his hand, "not so quick with the celebration. We still have a dinner show tomorrow, confirmation that Cecilia and Marty make their flight, and then our own extraction. We have work to do."

Dad was right but mom finished with, "There is champagne for all in the kitchen. Phase one is done and we need to take a minute to enjoy the big and little victories as they come. Meeting adjourned to the kitchen!"

FIFTY-FOUR

Houston OPS

- Cecilia and Marty were successfully extracted from Houston. The escape team is almost to their first destination. New identities will be arranged there.
- Dinner arrangements are ready for tonight's dinner. Ricardo and parents plus Cecilia's parents plus the governor and his wife will attend.
- Emmy will need to return to her apartment to prepare for her journey home. She should be packed and ready to leave before the dinner, in the event things go sideways. Because of Caesar running out on her, she will have a bodyguard escort arranged and demanded by her parents. All this is for show, so make it seem real.
- Whitey and Big bird will be driven to Ellington Air Force Base for a flight home immediately after the dinner.
- The real residents of the house that Whitey and Big bird used were delayed in Phoenix due to an intentional mix up with their tickets, so they will not arrive until late Monday.

FIFTY-FIVE

Dinner and Home

SUZANNE AND I ARE AT the apartment, packing. She's not going anywhere, and will be in the apartment for the summer while I'm gone. "Suzanne, I'm so glad you are going to be here. I feel like I pack up and move all the time."

Suzanne is so wonderful and such a great sounding board. "Hey, what's up with Charlie? I know you know, because it feels job-related. He seems anxious."

Suzanne closes the last suitcase and sits on the end of the bed. "Look, it's good you can read him. It's a sign that you two know each other well. He's worried about tonight. But, believe it or not, he does have a job that has responsibilities other than just your family. It's probably some other thing. He'll talk to you when he's ready. I can see how much he cares about you."

Suzanne is so careful with words all the time, I know there is something in that message I should notice. Then it hits me, "Is there a reason you used the word 'care' and not the word 'love'? Is there a problem that you know of?" Suzanne stiffens. "Come on, tell me what is going on?"

Suzanne stares off away from me. "I really don't know about any problem. I have, like you, noticed that he's been anxious. I hadn't thought it had anything to do with you until just now, when you made me think about it. Let's get through tonight and go from there. I'll be in the house tonight if you need me, just out of sight."

With that small reassurance, Suzanne and I move my luggage to the door just as Charlie lets himself in. "Well, hi. How are my two favorite girls doing?" Charlie leans in and kisses me while simultaneously picking up my suitcases to load to the car. Suzanne and I roll our eyes at each other and follow him out.

Thirty minutes later, we arrive at the house in River Oaks where the dinner is being held tonight. People here are on a mission. Besides the normal business of preparing dinner and housekeeping, there are techies and small meetings going on everywhere. I sit in on the one about the script for tonight and the three different scenarios. I'm to be distressed, betrayed and confused. This should make others feel that they need to console me and explain away the situation. We're hopeful that my performance will bring emotions in to the mix, and Ricardo or Cecilia's parents will make mistakes.

The governor and his wife arrive, and mom, dad and a few others debrief them in the living room. It's quick and like me they are instructed on what to do in the event that violence erupts. Two vehicles pull into the driveway, one limo and one black suburban. The expected guests unload along with four men who are immediately checked for weapons. The obvious weapons that are found are put in the back of the suburban. Charlie warned me that they probably had others, hidden well.

Ricardo and his crew are just inside the door when the Quinteros emerge from their limo. The absence of Cecilia and Marty has not been noticed yet. Showtime... I'm on.

"Ricardo, where is Caesar?" Ricardo's look says it all. "I have no idea. He left with you. I have not seen him since then."

I turn to dad and mom, "Mom, Dad, Caesar isn't with Ricardo and he didn't answer the phone at his place. I'm worried. He always checks in."

The conversation stops as Mr. and Mrs. Quintero, and Cecilia's younger sister Marta, step through the door. Ricardo is agitated but politely greets all. Marta comes over and speaks quietly to me, "Where is Cecilia? She said she was going to talk to you about spending the summer with you."

I'm surprised that she is asking about Cecilia. "Uhhhh. We were going to talk today about her summer plans and mine. She never spoke to me about coming with me to my home. She's not here with me."

At that second, it felt like a bomb of voices exploded around me.

"Where is Cecilia?"

"She isn't with you?"

"Why don't you know where she is?"

Angry voices are quelled when dad steps out into the middle of the foyer and asks everyone to step into the dining room so we can figure out what is going on. The governor and his wife move to the front door, "We're excusing ourselves from your family emergency, but please know that my office can help in any way needed. Just make the call and we'll make it happen."

Sean escorts them to their vehicle while the rest of our angry mob retreats to the dining room.

Dad starts with, "Let's get a timeline. When and where was the last time anyone saw Cecilia or Marty?"

Sean entered the room as the question is asked. "I saw Marty here when I got back from your place, Ricardo. I was coming in as he was leaving here. He said he had to talk to you and would be back later. I got sleepy from the long day and went to bed. He never returned, according to the man on duty at the gate. I figured he stayed with you."

Mr. Quintero shouted, "We left our Cecilia in your care, Ricardo. She was just fine when we left. What have you done with her?" Mrs. Quintero is sobbing into a handkerchief.

Marta snickers, "I bet she ran away from all of this. She hates this kind of stuff. I, on the other hand, think this is fun. I wouldn't worry. She will return when her money runs out."

The room explodes again with a lot of pointing and yelling. Sean, who had left the room, comes back in and adds to the cacophony by saying, "Excuse me. I sent out a BOLO on Caesar's car and it has already been located at Hobby airport. Apparently, he and a female passenger left yesterday evening on a Southwest flight to Atlanta with a connecting flight to Madrid."

If I had thought it was loud before, I was wrong. The roof could have blown off the house and this still would have been louder. Mr. and Mrs. Quintero and Ricardo's parents stand and head for the front door. Marta is pleading to stay and help Ricardo.

Ricardo is shaking off the teenage girl clinging to his arm.

Her dad has her other arm and there is a short tug of war, with Mr. Quintero winning. He drags her to the door and with a long spew of Spanish aimed at Ricardo, he is out the door and his little group practically jog to the limo.

Ricardo is not quite alone because his men, all four are standing by the door ready to go, when Ricardo pulls a gun. The place goes dead quiet. At that crazy moment, I decide to sob and wail uncontrollably. Mom comes to my side. Ricardo's men freeze. They look from one to the other and realize this is going bad. The biggest and oldest man steps forward and, with a boss-like voice, yells, "Ricardo, eres estupido? Tenemos que irnos ahora." Even I know he's called Ricardo stupid and says to leave, now.

Ricardo lifts his gun and two shots ring out. One from Ricardo, which hits the big man in the forehead, and the other from Sean, which hits Ricardo. Both men drop to the floor. I'm grabbed from behind and practically flung out of the room. Mom, dad and everyone else have weapons aimed at the remaining men and are taking cover waiting for the other three to fire. Instead, they drop their weapons raise their hands high in the air.

There's a little bit more chaos as the three men are cuffed. The big man is definitely dead and Ricardo is seriously injured. I hear Dad call "clear" and I peak around the door where Suzanne has me shielded. The three cuffed men are escorted outside and gone in minutes. An ambulance arrives and I can tell that Ricardo is touch and go. I stay back against the wall and just watch, there's nothing I can do. The ambulance will get him to the Med Center, which is no more than ten minutes away.

Five or six men come out of the woodwork and go with him to the hospital. We all move to the kitchen where there is food ready to be served. Dad and mom encourage everyone to make a plate and eat. "The food is excellent. We all have had a long day and a longer night ahead, so eat now while you have a minute. Big Bird and I will be on our way in one hour. Kitten and Charlie will need an escort to IAH Intercontinental Airport Houston."

My head pops up and I make eye contact with Charlie. He gets a plate and asks me to join him in the den. I grab a plate and follow. "IAH? What is that all about?"

He sets his plate down and explains, "I have another assignment I'm needed on. I have to board another flight as soon as I put you on the flight to Dulles. You will be met there and driven home. Your car will be garaged here until you get back. Doug Ballantine has agreed to lock it in one of the garages here. My flight is in a different direction."

I can't look at him. I'm sure I'd cry and that is the last thing I'm going to do with this audience. "How long?" is all I can manage.

"The assignment is like all assignments, it has variables. Best case scenario, a week, worst case, a month."

Emotionally, I'm done so eating isn't happening. I stand and tell him I'm ready to go. I just need a moment in the restroom and I'll meet him outside. I'm up and at the door of the kitchen waving to mom and dad, "See you two at home soon. Leaving my car here like you wanted, so please have something ready for me to drive when I land. Love you." I try to make that last statement sound as pleasant as I am sad.

I bound up the stairs and into the room I had slept in. You would never even know I had been there. Someone had been here and put it all in order. My things were even packed for a quick getaway if it had been needed. I went into the bathroom, sat down and cried. I know things change all the time but I just needed a good cry. I washed my face and left a thank you note on Doug's desk. I know he really had no choice but I wanted him to know I appreciated it. I really don't know him. We stood next to each other on Derby Day stuff, but that was all.

Ten minutes later, I have myself together. I've washed my face and combed my hair and I'm ready to go. To my surprise, Suzanne is with Charlie in the car, plus a driver. No alone time here. Great.

"Hi Suzanne, are you off to an assignment, too?" She looks away shyly. I know there's my answer, an answer I should already know but Charlie neglected to tell me. "Okay, let's be adults here, even if I don't get treated that way often. At least today, you two can try."

Charlie moved closer to me, "This is my fault. I knew about this assignment a few days ago and so did Suzanne. Suzanne knew because she is taking my place at the training. I will go later. I thought I would get a private moment to talk to you. Every time we were alone, I knew that you needed to focus and not be distracted by us, so I let it slide. Now, I regret that. Suzanne has scolded me over and over. I should have listened."

"Great… You can talk to Suzanne about our relationship but not me. That really helps." I know that was harsh but it is how I feel. I'm the little girl who can't have adult conversations because she'll fall apart. "When exactly will I be an adult in your eyes?"

There is no immediate answer. Suzanne broke the silence, "I, for one, think you can handle anything. I've read your file from front to back and you are one tough cookie. I'm going to D.C. with you not as your chaperone, but because I need to go to Langley for a class. We'll be on the same flight and have seats together, but when we land, you will go one way and I will go another."

Charlie was quiet. He reaches for my hand. I longed for him to be closer but I was not pushing myself onto someone who couldn't talk to me about simple things.

Charlie scoots over closer and speaks softly. "Emmy, this is my job. I get assignments. It will always be like this. I'm sorry I didn't let you know as soon as I knew. This will happen again and again, so you need to trust me."

He's right and I lean up against him so I can at least have the duration of the ride with him. I'll miss him. "I get that you work and it will take you from me. I would prefer to hear it from you and not in a meeting. When that happens, it feels like I'm your work. At one time, I was your job, but I feel like we have left that behind. I hope so anyway."

I know the driver and Suzanne can hear, but I just don't care. The last twenty minutes are heavenly kisses and it is so nice to finally be near him, sort of alone. Well, as alone as we can have for now.

The airport is busy and Charlie is being dropped at terminal A, and Suzanne and I will go on to terminal B. I get out with him so I can squeeze in one last kiss, at least for a while. Suzanne and I have plenty of time before our flight so the driver isn't concerned about the small delay. He makes the loop around to terminal B and drops us off. Our flight isn't full and I'm tired, so I sleep. Suzanne rouses me just as we are making our decent into Dulles International Airport. This is one of three airports in the metropolitan area around Washington, D.C.

"Emmy, our orders are to wait at baggage claim. Our drivers will both be there waiting." I know they all still think of me as a job, and technically I am, but it still bothers me. "Yes, I was given the same directive. I can handle this. I am not a child even though I get treated that way."

I can see I have hit a sensitive place with Suzanne. "You know, I just was making normal conversation, like a friend." My head whips back around to her. "A normal girlfriend would have said, "I was told that our rides will be waiting for us at baggage claim. What did you hear? Not tell me what the orders were. Small difference in words but big difference in meaning. I like you, Suzanne, but please don't patronize me."

Suzanne sighs, "You might be right. I don't have any adult girlfriends, just colleagues. And in college and high school, I was a nerd and into studying. I had few friends then. Sorry."

I roll my eyes, resigned at my need to cut her a break. "I understand, no apologies needed. You're just doing your job. It just gets old sometimes. It sure is good to have one of you guys around when things go bad, so I shouldn't gripe."

Since the plane is not full, it's a quick unload and baggage claim is pretty quiet. I spot the two drivers immediately and head their way. Suzanne grabs my arm, "Stop, something is up. Let's disappear into the restroom while I make a call. The one driver has his hands positioned in the warning signal."

I look again and she is right, the older man had his arms straight down and his fingers crossed. I've known about that warning signal since I was twelve, I just missed it. Thank goodness Suzanne saw it. I wonder what's up?

After checking the bathroom over, Suzanne leaves to use the pay phone and returns with good news. There was a suspicious person that was being questioned by the locals as a precaution.

We arrived as they had just begun the vetting. The agent was just choosing to be super cautious.

Just when I think I know what's next, this tall, handsome, young man comes towards us and scoops up Suzanne. "Suzy, I've missed you." He kisses her and whispers, "You two were followed from Houston. Play along with me." Suzanne giggles and turns to introduce me to him. "Emmy, this is my boyfriend, Frank. He arranged for someone to take you home so we can have some alone time. I hope you don't mind?"

Sure enough, just behind Frank there is an older man. Frank half turns, "This is my Uncle Fred and he's your ride."

As we walk out to the curb, I can see both men watching everything and everyone. I wasn't anxious when I got off the plane, but I am now. What else could go wrong? Why did I even think that? Don't press your luck, Emmy.

"Thanks, Fred. I will be so happy to get home. You're an angel to help out." Fred opens the door to a sleek black Cadillac and I get into the passenger seat. He goes to the trunk and loads my luggage. We have an hour drive from Dulles to Georgetown if there's not too much traffic. Fred hands me a note from Suzanne which reads, "Here is my home number and a message center number at the farm if you need me. Take care."

After we get on the highway, I turn to Fred. "Fred, who was following us?" His eyebrows lift but he doesn't take his eyes off the road. I'm talking about on the plane, but his answer spooks me. "Please don't turn around and look, but they still are. Suzanne and Frank are following them. We don't want to tip them off just yet."

I really want to turn around but I know better. "Who and why?" I'm at a loss as to who and why. Still looking straight ahead, Fred says "word on the street in Houston is that Old Man Quintero, you know Cecilia's father is having you watched because he thinks you are going to meet up with Cecilia and Caesar. You know, that you were in on it. That's what we want them to think. So they won't worry about either side staying close to you."

My brain just can't handle much more. "So, I'm bait again? Do my parents know?"

"Yes and yes. Again, please don't turn around but there is another agent in the car on the back seat lying down just in case they decide they want to talk to you themselves. We won't let that happen."

I really want to turn around, but instead I start looking out the rearview window on my side of the caddy.

"Oh, when we get close to your home, we will have the D.C. police pull them over for a broken tail light that they have now. That will delay them long enough to get you in the house without too many issues. Cops are just going to check IDs and write a warning."

I have seen that in the movies, someone takes out a headlight without reason other than to harass someone, "So did you help them to the broken tail light or what?"

The back seat spoke, well the agent in the back seat, "No, that was me. Michael McGuiness at your service."

We are about five blocks from home when we see the blue lights and Fred slows a bit and taps his breaks. "Emmy, if you want to look this is a good time to do that. These two men, wait it's a man and a woman, are busy."

I turn to look and my mouth drops open, "Holy cow! That is Mae Vicinti. What is she doing here? Let Houston know asap. They did a complete vet on her. She had her own agenda then; I don't know what it is now. I'm pretty sure she knew Marty was not Caesar. I don't know what deal she had with us but she did. I don't recognize the man."

I could hear Michael on the phone with Langley and he spit out a different route to Fred who immediately changed course. Michael tossed a bullet proof vest over the seat at me and said, "Put it on."

It still looks like we are heading home but not the front door as planned. I knew this was not the time to distract these two agents. They were being fed instructions as we flew down the street. Fred quickly turns down the alley behind our house and the garage door opens and he pulls inside. Before the door is closed completely Sean and dad are at the door to the house, guns drawn, signaling to come quickly, which I do.

Fred, Michael and me are hustled into the kitchen. Mom is

on the phone and hands it over to Sean. Sean turns and starts a barrage of questions at me. "Tell me all you know about Mae. Does Marty know her better? What about Sterling or Charlie? Did she ever get interviewed by Houston Ops? Who do you think she works for?"

I am happy to answer all of his questions but I think Marty would be better. "Houston Ops did interview her, but I was not there. Marty did spend time with her. Sterling and Charlie knew about her, I just don't know how much. She has some connection to the Klarsfeld movement in France. Mae was always nice to me but standoffish."

I sat down to listen and think if I knew anything else. Sean is back on the phone. Fred is on another other phone. Agent McGuiness went out the front door to see if that car had been released by DC police and had made it here.

Mom went to the window in the front of the house to watch Michael. She almost immediately came back to the kitchen. Michael was on her heels. "The car that was following us is parked just down the street on the other side. They're facing us. I'm calling it in." Michael starts for the phone but Sean intercepts him. "I relayed the message as you were speaking. Langley is on it."

What seemed like seconds later, but was really twenty minutes the doorbell rang. Everyone stopped dead. Mom headed for the door. Michael stopped her. "I got this. You now have a butler." I was told to stay put and I did. Everyone else moved to the front of the house with guns drawn. I can hear Michael open the door and greet whoever it is. There is a bit of a commotion and I'm sure I hear Mae's voice but I sit still.

Dad appears at the kitchen door with Sean behind him. "Emmy, this girl wants to talk to you and only you. She says you know and trust her. She is unarmed and there are five of us who think this is the most direct way to find out what is going on. Langley specialists are on the way. Play dumb." I roll my eyes, again with the play dumb thing.

"Sure... I'm good at young and dumb." Dad needed a reminder that I've been subjected to this crazy world for almost a year now but now wasn't the time to get into that. I took off the bullet proof vest, straightened my hair and headed for the living room.

"Hi Mae. What are you doing in D.C.? I thought you would be in Houston, working for Ricardo."

She jumped up, ready to give me a piece of her mind but when she did all five took a step towards her and she immediately sat. "Okay, I'm not going to hurt you. Stand down, everyone. I know that Emmy knows where Caesar, well, Marty, is and I need to know."

I took a seat across from her, "Why do you think that? Why do you need to talk to Marty? What makes you think I know where he is? He left me high and dry in Houston. Who are you working for?"

Mae looked at everyone then back to me. "I guess there's no chance I can talk to you alone." She looked back at everyone again, "Yea, I figured that. First, I never worked for that pig, Ricardo. Second, I'm glad Cecilia got away from him. He's abusive. I work for myself."

"So, let me get this straight. You work for yourself, which is for what cause or purpose. Or are you paid?" I know there are better questions but I can't think of any more. Sean comes to the rescue. "Emmy, I'd advise you not to answer any of Mae's questions without proof of who she is and what she wants that information for."

Mae begins, but stops midsentence as four agents, two men and two women, enter from the kitchen. One approaches and introduces himself and the others to her.

"Mae, I believe you and the Houston Office have a verbal and written agreement in regard to Mr. Ricardo Moreno, his group and the Quintero family. Is that correct?"

"Yes, that is correct, in part. I agreed to check in with Caesar, a.k.a. Marty, and that is what I'm attempting to do. Marty said if I could not talk to him, find Emmy and she would always have access to him. I'm here for that and only that."

This agent didn't even miss a beat. "I'm here. I'm her access to Marty. She has no idea where he is. We are looking for him, too. He is off the grid at present. We expect to hear from him in due time."

Mae is not one to be pushed aside, I know that much. So, I

was not surprised when she turns back to me, "Emmy, I want to hear your voice and not these paid bodyguards and bureaucrats. Is that the truth? You really don't know where he is?"

Sean begins to speak, but Mae puts her hand up to stop him. "Emmy, I'm not here to cause problems. I need to talk to Marty. The Quintero family reached out to me to assist in finding Cecilia since Ricardo is out of the picture."

This information about Ricardo is news to me. "Why is Ricardo out of the picture? I know that he was shot, but it didn't kill him, right?"

Mae looks from me to the others. "This is why I'm talking to you and not them. Ricardo is going to be in the hospital and assisted living for a while because of the injury to his spine from the ricocheted bullet. He will never walk again. That is not good when you need to be the tough guy. He is not smart so a desk job is not for him either. Hence, he's out of the picture. His little group sort of fell apart. If Caesar was there, he could take over, but he has to give Cecilia back."

All I can say is "Wow!"

Agent McGuiness came over and sat next to me and looked directly at Mae. "Mae, I get why you want to talk to Emmy, because you can tell if she is telling the truth or not. She has not been trained to hide her emotions and is therefore readable. No offense, Emmy. But she really doesn't know where he is. I think your gut tells you that. If we knew where he was right this minute, we still wouldn't tell her for her own safety. I have an idea to propose to you."

Mae gives him the wide-eyed, chin down universal look of *really*. "Go ahead, I'm listening."

Agent McGuiness is not deterred, "You and Emmy come with us to Langley and talk. You are not under arrest or being detained by our government. Just some straight talk about your mission and Marty. Emmy's parents will accompany us for her protection and their peace of mind."

Mae looks resigned and worried. I decide to just get her to make a decision so that this tense moment ends. "So, Mae what do you think? I'm game, how about you?"

Mae appears to be struggling with an internal issue, but with my question she came back with an answer. "Okay, Emmy. I will ride with you in a car. I have a concern that must be addressed first. In the car outside your home is a man assigned to me by Señor Quintero. I don't trust him with what I will learn and, for sure, you do not want him at Langley with us. I don't want him to get suspicious of my loyalty and question my purpose here."

McGuiness turns to two of the agents who had just arrived. "You two, go get him and make sure you are firm that he is being detained for questioning. Put him in your car but make sure he can see the front door of this house. We will escort Mae out in cuffs so he can see she is being detained, too. Emmy, you go around to the garage and get in the car ahead of time so this guy doesn't see that you are with Mae. Will that work Mae?"

Mae nods. I'm so surprised to see that McGuiness took charge and no one questioned his authority, even mom and dad. A few minutes later everything is in place. Mom and dad, with Sean, are on their way to Langley. I'm in a car heading around to the front of the house to pick up Mae. Agent McGuiness comes out with Mae in tow and the people in the other car watch as we depart. Mae chances a look at her hired partner, just to assure herself he saw her.

In the car, Mae asks, "Where will you take him? Surely not Langley."

McGuiness looks over his shoulder from the front seat, "We have a special place for interviews. He will see you go in ahead of him and then he will go in. Our vehicle will go around the corner of the building out of site and pick you back up for a short drive to the main building. He'll think you are both at the same place."

"Will you interrogate him?" I ask this because I know Mae would want more info. McGuiness answers me, "Yes, but not as a hostile guest, just fact finding. He probably won't be too forthcoming, but we will tell him what we know about him and his connections to Quintero and see what he says. You never know. He might be unhappy with his boss and want out. If he does, we'll work a deal if we can and tell him Mae will not be the wiser."

I lean back and relax. I didn't even realize how tense I was.

Mae leans back, too, and closes her eyes. I wish I knew what she was thinking, and her true agenda. Her contacts with the Nazi hunters in France and her interest in the real Caesar have me wondering if my parents are in danger from her or if they're on the same side. Hopefully, we'll know soon.

Langley always fascinates me. This time, I'm much deeper in the building than in the past and I'm sure I look like a deer in the headlights. I follow, with my mouth closed and my eyes open, to a comfortable meeting room where I find mom, dad and Sean. Suzanne is here for me. To use her words, "I'm here for you so that you're comfortable." Mae wanted me here for her comfort, and mom and dad were here for their peace of mind. Why was I here? Oh yeah, as the bait and middle-woman, I guess.

Mom, dad and Sean have folders in front of them which I figure are all about Mae and who she is, what she knows and what she seems to want. Mom ends the silence.

"Mae as you know, I'm Emmy's mom, and her dad and I are foremost concerned with her safety. Our jobs are not her job, but for some unforeseen circumstances she has been dropped into the mix. We are here to listen and protect her. What is your involvement in the Klarsfelds of France?"

Mae definitely was not expecting that question at all and it shows on her face. She took everyone in before she spoke. "I know both Serge and Beate Klarsfeld, and believe in their mission as if it were my own. I provide the Klarsfelds with any intel that I feel will assist them in finding and apprehending any Nazi and or sympathizers. These Nazi need to be brought to justice."

Dad speaks next, "Have you found any that you have reported on while you've been here in the U.S.?"

"Not really. I came here from Spain to New York City, following Maximus and Carlos Ramos. They are part of the supposedly disbanded Rat Line. The Klarsfelds know this group still exists in Spain and Italy but need intel on them. The Ramos brothers got here then disappeared before I could set up surveillance on them. I'm not sure where they went or for what purpose, but I bet you know. I recognized Emmy in New York from Spain. She didn't remember me because I was never out in the open for her to meet. I'm not here to hurt her, but as you say due to some unforeseen circumstances she has landed smack dab in the middle of this."

At this point, the door opens to the meeting room and a group of four agents file in. One is Agent Michael McGuiness. He takes the lead and gets things started. "I hope everyone is comfortable. If anyone needs anything, let me know." One of the men is setting up a screen of some sort like he is going to show home movies. Looks interesting.

"I see some of you have briefing folders but, for the record, let's state what we're here for and what we know. Let's start with you, Mae. Can you tell us what your visit to the U.S. is all about?"

"Like I told Emmy and her parents, I came here from Spain following Maximus and Carlos Ramos. They are part of the supposedly disbanded Rat Line. The Houston Ops was apprised of that. The Klarsfelds know this group still exists in Spain and Italy but need intel on them. The Ramos brothers got here, then disappeared before I could figure out what they were up to. I'm not sure where they went and to what purpose, but I'm sure you know."

"What made you go to Houston?" McGuiness asked.

"I followed Emmy to Washington D.C. from New York, and then on to Houston. I knew about Ricardo Moreno in Houston and how he has his finger on the pulse there so I made contact. When I heard in his social circle that he was meeting up with Caesar, I was seriously interested so I got invited to dinner with them. I was so surprised when I walked into the restaurant and saw Emmy."

"Did your mission change after that?" McGuiness asked.

"Not really, it just got a little more complicated when Ricardo introduced Marty as Caesar and I knew he was not the real Caesar but a damm close imposter." Mae is resigned at this point to just tell it all. "Marty and I met with some of your buddies in Houston and I agreed to keep up the ruse as long as I was kept in the loop about the Rat Line and Nazis. That is really it in a nutshell. One of the guys in Ricardo's group told the Quinteros that I had good connections in the world market of intel and so here I am."

McGuiness smiles and picks up the phone in front of him. A few words later in French, he hands the phone to Mae. She looks puzzled but takes the phone. Her expression changes to a genuine smile. She listens and recites a short nursery rhyme. There were a few nods of her head and yes sirs but mostly Mae just listens. She hands the phone back to McGuiness and he says 'thank you' and gives a cordial goodbye before hanging up.

Mae starts the conversation first this time, addressing my mom and dad. She stands, extending her hand to them. "It's an honor to meet the two of you. Serge Klarsfeld just explained who you two are and what you do. No wonder you are careful with Emmy and protect her, especially when someone like me pops into the picture. I am so sorry if I was a source of worry. I would never touch Emmy in a harmful way. I will do whatever you think needs to be done without question."

That seems too easy, but it works because everyone starts to lay out a plan that doesn't include me and I'm not envious at all. I'm ready for a quiet, relaxing summer break. I could have gotten up and danced on the table and no one would have noticed if it hadn't been for Suzanne. She got up and moved over close.

"I saw a communication come in from Marty and they're okay. Thought you would like to know. I also got a worried call from Charlie wondering where you are and why you didn't pick up the phone at your house. I explained and he said he would call you in the morning."

I'm so grateful for her info. "Both great pieces of news. Thank you! Aren't you tired? Both of us have been on the road and moving since five this morning. This day just never ends," I sigh.

Suzanne winks and whispers "Watch this, I can fix that." Louder, she calls "McGuiness, a word." Agent McGuiness came over and Suzanne laid out her idea. "If the situation with Mae is handled, and it won't disrupt your planning meeting, I would like to move a very exhausted Emmy back to her home. I can stay with her until everyone else arrives home."

McGuiness looks at us, "You do both look tired. I guess this seems never-ending. I'll arrange for a car to take both of you back to the house and someone to stay so you can both close your eyes for awhile. Suzanne, you have a big day tomorrow so get some rest. No all-night girl talk, please." Both of us thank him and say our good byes and are whisked back to Georgetown. At this time in the evening, the roads are not too busy so it is a quick trip, about thirty minutes. I'm in the house, showered and in bed thirty minutes after I arrive home. After that, sleep is easy.

FIFTY-SIX

Langley OPS

- Make a file on the man accompanying Mae. Isolate him until we can get a plan in place for Mae. Houston needs to be apprised of all intel.
- Marty and Cecilia made it to their last destination for now. New identities are in place.
- With Mae's help, Kitten will be extracted from the Ricardo issues left over in Houston, hopefully for good.
- Sterling and Charlie are delayed.

FIFTY-SEVEN

Charlie

HOME IS A GREAT PLACE to be. I don't need to worry about who might turn up and be dangerous. At least, not in a Ricardo kind of way. Mom and dad have lots of social obligations when they're home. Lucy has a boyfriend, so they're busy. I'm not going to sit around and feel sad that Charlie's not at my side. He is still on assignment. If I want to be treated like an adult, I need to suck it up and endure his absence.

I like to go to the country club to swim and keep in shape at the gym for next year's dance team and cheerleading. The food at the club is good, too. Mom and dad meet friends there at least two to three times a week for dinner. One evening, mom approaches, "Emmy, your dad and I would like you to come along to dinner with us. We are eating dinner with friends. Two of the families will have college-age children with them. Lucy is in New York, but we'd like you to be with us. I hope you don't mind? You can come home after dessert, if it is too boring." Mom and dad rarely ask that I hang out with them so this must be important. "Sure mom, no problem. Is a summer dress okay for tonight?"

Mom's answer is her standard, "Whatever you wear will be perfect. We need to leave in an hour."

Okay, I will just have time for a shower, hair and get dressed. As I head up the stairs, I call back to her, "Okay, mom. I'll be ready in one hour."

When we get in the car to go to the club, Mom tells me, "One of the college kids that will be with us tonight says he knows you. He said you met in Houston."

I can't imagine who I know in Houston that would be here in D.C. "That's interesting. Wonder who it is?"

Mom shrugs her shoulders, "I didn't get a chance to ask, we were interrupted. So, it will be a surprise for both of us."

"Great," is all I can think… Surprises and me have not gone well lately. The club is packed. I'm not here in the evenings typically, so this is all new for me. The dining area is to the right as you come up the large entry stairs to the first floor. Below this floor is the pro shop, locker rooms, gift shop and small snack bar. It's open during the day and closes at seven on weekdays. Besides the dining room, there's a ballroom on the left used for meetings and parties, plus a lovely balcony the stretches across the whole back wall looking out over the golf course.

We're early, dad thinks fifteen minutes early is on-time, but we manage to get seated. I like getting to pick out the seats we want. To my dismay, mom shares that the college kids are to sit at one end of the table so the old folks won't bore them. Dad sits at the head of the table, so I follow suit and sit at the other end of the table. He smiles and says, "Good choice. Always take the upper hand when you can."

I can tell the others are arriving when dad smiles, stands and starts greeting folks. A couple of them I know, so that's nice. One guy close to my age is introduced as Erik Matheson. He's studying business at the University of Maryland. He's around six feet tall and athletic. I can hear the reluctance in his voice that says he, too, has been instructed to come along. I guess this is 'show off your kid' night cause mom apologizes that Lucy could not make it, she had prior commitments. Erik looks at me, "so my brother bailed, too. I wasn't fast enough with an excuse so here I am. Looks like you and I have that in common."

He's right, but I'm not going to let him get away with making bold, baseless assumptions. "You know, my mom and dad rarely ask much of me, and they didn't force me tonight. They do so much for me that if they want me with them, it's the least I can do." Erik stammered and then got his bearings, "I didn't mean to imply that you didn't want to be here. I just figured that a beautiful woman like you would be out with your man or bring him along."

Just as I am about to speak, I get a kiss on the cheek. "Hey Derby girl... Glad you could come. You made my night." He reaches around and introduces him self to Erik. "Hi, I'm Doug Ballentine. I play golf at the same university that Emmy attends."

Oh no, this is the guy that lived in the house we used in River Oaks. The golfer that I was assigned to make a derby for. Doug sits down on my right and Erick is on my left. Before I can respond Doug continues, "Thanks for the derby. It's hanging in my room. Oh, but you would have seen it when you stayed in my room last weekend." Erick is looking at me like someone other than the nice girl he had just been talking to. I'm sure I'm blushing.

We're interrupted by the waiter with water and asking what we want for drinks. In D.C., the drinking age is eighteen and I sure need a glass of wine. The other two follow suit. No one at the table is paying us any mind, which is good. I turn to Erik and put my hand on top of his, "Yes, I decorated his derby hat for a fundraiser, and I did spend two nights in his empty room while he was in Arizona." Erik put his other hand on top of mine and smiles a suggestive smile, "I like a woman who knows what she likes and doesn't worry about what it looks like."

Ewwww... I pull my hand out and hiss, "Stop being creepy. I did not spend the night with him. And you," I turn to Doug, "you need to set this story right. If not, both of you will be wearing your food, or drinks, or both." You know how sometimes a space gets quiet at the wrong time? Well it did, and everyone heard my last two sentences. Everyone has identical scrunched eyebrows like they smell something foul and are trying not to show it on their face.

To Doug's credit, he speaks and fills the void with a gracious answer, "This is my fault. I was teasing Emmy without considering how it sounded to an outsider. She has every right to be angry. I hope she will accept my apology." He is looking straight at me. I nod and smile, and the tension in the air subsides. What else could I do? I really want to drop food in their laps, but now everyone would not understand if I did. Erik, not to be outdone, also offers an apology. Thank goodness everyone else went back to their conversations. I look back and forth between both young men and decide I'll just eat and get out of here as soon as possible.

I have been to so many dinners like this with older adults and have learned to listen and engage in semi-meaningful conversations. Tonight would be no different. I try to join in with the nearest adults, and they're polite but not too interested in welcoming a child into their conversation. This means I have these two idiots to engage with.

By the time dessert arrives, both Erik and Doug have settled into talking about college and their personal goals. I listen politely, as I've be taught to do, but I'm ready to bolt given any opportunity.

I can hear music drifting in from the area just outside the dining room. I have never had occasion to be there, so I didn't know that this country club has its own version of a bar/club. Erik notices my interest. "Emmy, do you dance?" I don't get a chance to answer because Doug answers for me. "You bet, she dances. She's the cougar mascot for the University of Houston, and on their dance team the Houston Honey's, not to mention she danced for two years on American Bandstand plus some other TV dance show in Baltimore."

Erick's not deterred by Doug's revelation that he knows a lot about me, "I just asked because I thought you might want to get away from the folks and dance." My head swivels around to take in both guys. One wants to dance… I like that… One has clearly done research on me… I'm not sure I like that or know how to process it. So, dancing it is. At least it will thankfully get me away from my parent's friends without another scene. Dancing will also make it easier to duck out, head home away from these two.

Erick stands and offers a hand. My dad's chin turns just enough to see where we are headed. Doug follows.

Okay, progress I can work with. Now, I have two to ditch instead of the ten others at the table. I can do this.

Erick can dance, Doug cannot. After a few dances, and my second drink not counting the glass of wine from dinner, we wander out to the balcony that looks over the golf course. Other than the moon above and the lights from this building, it is really dark in front of us. Doug stands on my right, "Peaceful, isn't it?" He's right, it is. During the day though, the area below us is seriously busy with golfers and the like.

"It's peaceful for now, but early tomorrow morning it will be like a hornet's nest down there." Erick, who is to my left, says, "Doug, I understand you're a dang good golfer. When's your next tournament?" Doug doesn't miss a beat, so you can tell he has had this question asked many times before. "I have a U.S. Open qualifier next weekend here. Kind of nice since this is like my home course. And then the U.S. Open. I hope to place high in the Open. My coach at U of H expects all of us on the team to do well. I want to be the best."

I guess Doug is good at what he does because the two of them talk for a while about golf as if I'm not here. I didn't see Sean approach and I don't think the guys did either because they sort of jumped when he speaks. "Emmy, your parents are having the car brought around. Will you be leaving with them?" I turn and nod at him. He extends an elbow and I take it, all the while saying goodnight.

A few feet away I tell Sean, "Thank you for rescuing me. I'm sure those young men are okay but I miss Charlie and I'm not in the mood to pretend to be interested."

"Your dad said to check on you and offer you a way out if you wanted it. I'm glad to help. With that said, I have news that you will not be happy about. Charlie will not be here for awhile, definitely not until after the Fourth of July. I think you should find something to keep you busy." He's right. I can't even think of anything to say so I nod. What can I do that will keep me busy, mentally and physically?

The next couple days I try to set up a routine so that I don't just live in my room. The country club has a lot going on every day. My parents are home for the next few weeks so I take advantage of having time with them. Mom likes to play cards at the club and dad plays golf.

Mom is easy to spend time with. She plays canasta and it's an easy game to learn. Golf, on the other hand, is not so easy. I mean, I'm coordinated so I hit the ball most of the times. I just hit it really good one time, then awful the next. I'm used to being successful at most everything physical I do. Dad and I do play golf, but not with his buddies, just the two of us. I have only made it nine holes with him so far. Dad shows me where the range is to practice and I take the hint and decide I need a little time there each day. It's a good, repetitive use of most of my muscles so I'm there instead of the gym. I guess Doug is there too, but busy in his competitive world. I haven't seen him but I'm not looking for him either.

I had just finished a bucket of balls and start packing up to leave late one afternoon when he approaches. "Hey Emmy, wait up. Where are you headed?" Doug is cute and, according to Sean, he's wealthy and is headed to life as a professional golfer. I look up and he's less than a foot from me. "I'm heading home. Dad is out on the course and mom already left. I came with dad, so I can wait up there on the balcony and watch for him to come in at eighteen from there. Why what's up?"

He points at a beautiful, customized golf cart that is definitely his and says, "I'm going to get in a quick nine, want to play?"

I raise eyebrow and lower my chin in an expression that needs no words but I voice them anyway. "Really? For you, it would be like a pro playing with a toddler."

"Come on, just for fun. I'll swing left-handed to even the odds."

"I am not a betting person, especially when I haven't a chance of winning. Besides I have seen you switch hit. You can swing both ways."

That was a stupid thing for me to stay, but there's no way to back out of admitting that I had watched him. I didn't even think about the alternate meaning of "swing both ways."

Doug grins. "I like that you've been watching me. Please, if you're going to say I swing both ways, make sure people are clear you mean golf because I'm only attracted to women."

I step back and stammer, "I hadn't even considered that thought." Truth be told, I could not think of a person I know who is gay. I guess I still have things to learn. He took my clubs and headed for the cart.

Maybe if I swing in front of him, he can tell me why sometimes

I hit the ball and others I don't. Nothing like free lessons. He straps my bag on to the back of the cart and off we go. We start at the at one and are planning to try to get nine before the sun goes down. As we approach the ninth tee, I can see Sean waiting. He arrived in a cart. I hope there is nothing wrong. "Emmy, your dad needs to leave now. I will send someone to get you shortly. He is not going home, so you can't come with us."

Doug hops out of the cart and walks up to Sean, "I can get her home if that's okay? I know you guys checked me out long ago and found I'm harmless." Sean chuckled, "I wouldn't say harmless, but that's up to Emmy."

There is a moment's pause while I thought over my options... Go home now and be alone, or stay. I've enjoyed talking to Doug, and at home I'd be bored.

"Sean, Doug can get me home. You concentrate on Dad." Sean didn't hesitate as he takes off up the fairway toward the parking lot.

"Let's play this last hole, grab a bite and then I can take you home. I'm starved. I need some calories."

For the next three weeks, every day Doug and I play nine just as the course starts to clear for the day. Even though we use a cart, I'm still getting good exercise and becoming a much better player. Dad and I occasionally play and he notices the big improvement. I'm sure he is aware that Doug is teaching me. Nothing is secret in my life.

The biggest secret in my life is where Charlie is and when will he be back. He doesn't call. I assume because he can't. When he's been gone before, he called, not often but he calls. This lack of contact is heart-sickening. My mind makes up stuff and I worry. Does everyone do that or am I weird? Will I always feel insecure when he is gone? Does this stop when you get older? When I get lost in those thoughts, I remember the nuns at the boarding school. Sister Claire in particular would say at least a thousand times a day, "Let go. Let God." Maybe that is what I should do? I am not outwardly religious but I'm definitely inwardly spiritual.

I'm still pondering life's problems when Doug arrives back to the table with sandwiches and drinks in hand. As far as rich privileged kids go, he has manners and seems nice. I've met some real strange ones along the way. Lunch is pleasant. I did notice that everyone knows him and wants to know who I am. I suppose he's always in the public eye and he seems okay with that scrutiny and… well, he's gracious. I decide to step farther in to his world. "Doug, you seem very comfortable in the limelight. That's a good quality to have in your line of work."

His response is, "It comes with the territory. Besides the golf, my parents have always drawn a crowd especially with all four of us boys with them. You get used to it. Just like you, with the bodyguard thing. You have this experience all the time, too. Today, however, this group is all into checking "us" out. This lunch thing will probably make the society column or the local sports review." I'm not so sure I see playing golf as a job, but he does that's for sure. I'm surprised at his knowledge of my personal situation with security. "The society page and sports review? Why?" My parents are in the news, socially, all the time so I get why for them. But Doug and I? Why?

He is quiet for a moment, then, "Well, both of us are considered eligible singles. You have political clout by way of your parents and I have money. If there was an 'us,' we would make a strong alliance. Politics and money always like each other. That lady who approached us first is a reporter. She specializes in the society column for The Post. Those two over by the wall are sports reporters here watching who is contending for an Open berth. That would be me and several others like my four teammates who are here for the qualifier next week.

He really does have a finger on the pulse of this place. I'm surprised. "I saw her take a photo, but now that you mention it, we would have been in the background."

He really laughs, "Wrong, we were the picture. Time to go. Too many vultures here."

His car is a 1971 Ford Torino GT, just what everyone is talking about and it's just a few months old. He did the gentlemanly thing and opened the door for me but to my surprise he also leaned in and pulled a black strap across my lap. He called it a seat harness. None of our cars has this. "Is this kind of seatbelt a new safety thing?"

As Doug is stretched across me, he stops to answer. "Yes, this cross-the-shoulder strap is kind of new, especially in fast cars. It also allows me a legitimate reason to get very close, so I can do this." With that, he kissed me. Full on the lips and not a sweet peck either. I didn't resist, but I didn't lean in either. As he releases me, "Mmmm, that was nice. Such tasty lips and you smell amazing. If we weren't in such a public place, I'd ask for more."

He backs out quickly and closes the car door. I can see in the rearview mirror that he is crossing to the driver's seat. I wasn't sure what to do. I couldn't jump out of the seat and run. That would cause a scene. I just didn't want to have that happen again. I felt like I had cheated on Charlie. I know I didn't initiate the kiss but I hadn't pulled back either.

Doug hopped in and pulled out. He turns out of the driveway and pulls over to the curb about a block from the club. "You haven't said a word. Have I pissed you off or are you so enamored with me you are speechless? I'm hoping somewhere in between."

He's right, he needs a response. So, here goes. Let's see if I can explain to him about Charlie and why I'm angry at myself. "Okay, you deserve the in-between reason. There's this guy."

He interrupts, "You mean the blonde I've seen you with on campus. I've seen you hold hands, I figured he was just playing a role to keep you safe. Or is it the dark Mediterranean looking guy? He seems into you, too. I don't see a ring."

I cut my eyes at him and he smiles. "Yes, I've been watching. I like what I see and want to see more of you. Bruce, one of my teammates, bet me I couldn't kiss you. It was a bet at first, but over these past weeks I've had plenty of opportunities to kiss you. I didn't want you to get angry and end our fun on the course."

This time I turn to face him, "So you won… Good for you. I don't like being the object of a bet. So, which team member is so insensitive so I can avoid him? Oh… And for the record, I'm not engaged to anyone. I am, however, in a serious relationship. He's working out West for a couple more weeks but should be here soon. I shouldn't have allowed you to kiss me. Your kiss was nice, but I feel like I have cheated on him."

His eyebrows went up, "Well if it makes you feel better, tell him I started it and you were a victim. I liked it and anytime you change your mind just step up and kiss me… I'd love that."

Doug pulled away from the curb and headed to my home. The rest of the short ride home was quiet.

When I step inside, I leave my clubs at the door. I can hear lots of talking in the kitchen, so I head in that direction. Right before I get to the door, I hear Charlie ask, "So, when do you think she'll be here? I have a mountain of paperwork to complete ASAP at Langley." I want to run into his arms, but I temper that urge due to the large number of people in the kitchen. A quick hug and a peck on the cheek is all he gets, for now. I'm trying to be mature. As I pull away, he takes my hand and excuses us from the group. I'm thrilled with the alone time, but I look at Sean as I pass him and I can see he's sad… I wonder why.

Charlie leads me to my room. I'm again more than happy to be there with him. He doesn't talk the whole way up the stairs, but I can see in his face as we pass the mirror in the hall. His jaw is locked and his expression is very serious.

He points to the bed for me to sit but I come close, step in and kiss him. It's a hungry kiss and he initially returns the kiss, but then suddenly stops. I can feel something is wrong. I sit on the edge of the bed, expecting him to join me. I pat the space beside me but I'm holding my breath without even realizing it. His next words stun me. "Emmy, there's no way to say this without hurting you. I've found someone else. I'm not going to lead you on when I know being with her is the right place for me to be. It's so right that I've resigned from my job."

I don't move. I have no words. My chest hurts. I want to cry but I don't. I know him well enough to know that this is hard for him. I sit so still that he comes and sits beside me. "Emmy, I will always care for you and if you ever need me, I will come. Please speak. Yell at me. Hit me, do something."

It takes a minute and several deep breaths to get myself steady enough to speak. It doesn't come out loud or angry. "I've missed you and will miss you. I can only hope that you're right in your decision. She's a lucky girl. You have made it very clear that it's time for you to close our chapter and start your new one. I have some crying to do, so please go."

Charlie starts to speak, but I put my finger on his lips and shake my head as tears run down my face. I stand. He stands. I guess he thought I was going to hug him but instead I turn and move around the bed and lay down. "Please go. I'll be okay. Tell Sean or whoever you told first not to bother me for a while. Thanks."

Charlie stood for a long moment then turns and leaves. Will I ever see him again? He took a piece of my heart with him. I cry, a lot. I don't know what else happened in the house that night. I cried and slept, and when I woke early the next morning the house is still. I seem to be alone. I shower, dress and make my way to the garage to the car that is mine for the summer. I have my swimsuit and two changes of clothes for later. Maybe a swim at the club would help clear my head.

I leave a note for my parents, *Mom, dad, I'm sure you're aware of Charlie's departure. I'm okay. I just need to drive and think. I'll call you later. Love Emmy.*

I turn into the parking lot at the club expecting to find a very busy place. Instead, the attendant tells me that the club is closed today to prepare for the Open qualifier and the Fourth of July celebrations. Okay, so no swimming here. I need to drive and think. I turn up the radio only to hear happy, summer fun music. After a few happy songs, a new one for the BeeGees, 'How can you Mend a Broken Heart' comes on. That's exactly what I need to know. The lyrics don't have an answer, but I do find myself crossing the four-mile long bridge on the Chesapeake Bay heading towards Ocean City, Maryland. I know where I'm headed. I'm heading to a place with happy memories. I hope my Aunt Dorothy's beach house isn't rented. I need a place to stay.

Just as I get over the bridge I pull over and find the nearest pay phone. First, to tell mom and dad where I am, and second to get my aunt's phone number. After a lot of explaining how I feel and where I am and what I want to do, mom says, "I will make the call for you. By the time you arrive in OC and stop at the realtor that handles the property, arrangements will be made. If it is not at Dorothy's, it will be another place so don't worry. I got this. Love you."

I hang up, add gas to the tank, get a drink for the road and return to the highway. During the middle of the week, it's not too busy on this road. On the weekend's, it's bumper to bumper, sometimes like a slow-rolling party.

Hours later, I cross the small bridge into Ocean City. The song blaring on the radio is Diana Ross singing, 'Ain't no Mountain High Enough.' She's setting me free and lifting my heart. I realize that people come and go in your life for a reason. You don't always get a choice of who you keep or for how long. This growing up thing is a process that I thought was a destination. I'm beginning to understand it's never-ending change.

Mom came through for me. The lady at the realtor's office gives me directions to a very nice hotel on the boardwalk, The Grand Hotel and Spa on Baltimore Street. I guess Aunt Dorothy's place was rented.

I let the valet park the car and go check in. The person at the desk is efficient and hands me keys to my room. As I turn towards the entrance to pick up my bag, I look up to see Doug standing in front of me. There are three other guys following him. He smiles big, "Hey Emmy. I like a girl who watches me, but it's even better when she follows me."

I lean in and surprise him with a kiss. One of the guys sputters, "You won!"

ABOUT THE AUTHOR

Cathy O'Bryan is a new author with 30 years experience in teaching Theatre, Art, and Competitive Speech and Debate. After years of reading, dissecting, and performing other works, she has ventured out on her own with this debut novel.